THE IMPOSSIBLE HORSE

CHRISTINE PULLEIN-THOMPSON

ISBN 978-1-914389-38-2

A NOTE ON THE TEXT

In *The Impossible Horse,* Jan and her friends and family use the pounds, shillings and pence system of money that everyone in Britain used until decimalisation in 1971. There were twenty shillings in a pound and twelve pennies in a shilling. Five shillings made a crown, which was a coin only released on special occasions, such as the Queen's coronation in 1953; half a crown was therefore two shillings and sixpence.

A pound in 1959 would be the equivalent of around £20 in 2023.

The text

The text is from the first edition, with no alterations. We have used the author's own name, rather than the pseudonym of Christine Keir, under which the book was originally published, as the book did appear under Christine's name as a later paperback.

Hunting was legal when this book was published, and it does, perhaps inadvertently, provide some solid arguments for banning hunting. Be warned that there is a particularly upsetting animal death scene in this book.

1

I SUPPOSE last winter was one of the most eventful in my life. Everything began on a wet December day with an east wind which cut through you like a knife, and a sky which promised nothing but more rain.

It was hardly a day for hunting, but hounds were meeting at Little Cross and nearly everyone would be there—by that I mean all the local people, Chris Miller, Guy Maunder, the Stanmore girls and their mother and a host of younger children and a collection of adults whom I knew by sight, but not by name, and, of course, the Master, Captain Williams.

I was seventeen and had just left school. As an experiment I was taking horses to break and school and at that time I had three in my stable, grey Fantasy, piebald Domino and an ugly black called

Velveteen. I lived with my parents in a plain stone Victorian house with a gable at each end, and old-fashioned stabling for four and a paddock.

On that morning, I rose early and lunged Fantasy before starting to groom Velveteen, whom I had decided to hunt. I remember his temper was even worse than usual and I wondered whether he would ever improve and be suitable for his owner, a woman called Miss Presscott.

The weather-cock above the stable pointed east when I hurried indoors for breakfast. Mummy was up and had put the kettle on. She and I are not very alike; she is small and dark with lovely hazel eyes, while I'm five foot eight and have flaxen hair. Often I wish I was smaller, so that I could school ponies; as it is, I can't take anything under fourteen two.

We made toast together, before Daddy appeared in a dressing-gown and said, "You're hunting today, aren't you, Jan? Be careful. The forecast says snow."

I said, "Okay. I shan't stay out too long. I'm taking Velveteen, and he isn't very fit."

Daddy is half Swede and has a great deal of hair, which in certain lights looks nearly white. He was invalided out of the Navy after the war with a wonky leg.

"Is that the horrid black?" asked Mummy.

"Yes, but he's much nicer now," I replied before I

dashed upstairs with a piece of toast in one hand and a mug of coffee in the other.

I changed quickly. I hadn't any hunting clothes and I put on jodhs, a polo-necked jumper, socks, shoes and a dark hacking jacket. My hat and hunting whip were in the hall. Mummy had made me cheese sandwiches. She kissed me.

"Do be careful," she said.

Outside sleet was falling. I thought of turning back for my mackintosh, but I hate hunting in one and there would be no one to take it from me at the meet. So I went on without it and fetched an eggbutt snaffle and a saddle from the tack-room and put them on Velveteen. He nearly bit me as I pulled up the girth, and his ears were back as I led him into the small Staffordshire-bricked yard.

Mummy called "Don't stay out too long" from an upstairs window as I rode out of the yard and Daddy opened the back door and called, "Have a good day."

The road to Little Cross looked bleak and cold and Velveteen jogged and threw his head from side to side. And now the sleet was falling in earnest and I wished that I had brought a spare pair of gloves.

The fields around us are open and fenced by cut and laid hedges and occasionally wire. But as you near Little Cross the landscape changes and there are friendly hills, beech woods, a winding river and thatched cottages. When I came to the first wood,

Velveteen seemed to settle down and there was shelter from the sleet and we both began to feel more cheerful. And presently I heard the sound of hoofs behind and hounds came round the corner gay and smiling. Tom the huntsman called, "Good morning, missy. What weather!" And somehow the scarlet coats, the jingling bits, the creak of leather seemed to dispel the bleakness of the day, and I felt like singing as we all rode on along the road together.

"What have you got today?" Tom asked.

"Miss Presscott's black. He's called Velveteen."

"Looks up to plenty of weight," said Tom.

The Stanmore girls were already at Little Cross when we arrived. Audrey, the eldest, was mounting a chestnut with three white socks, Susan was on her usual roan, and Sonia the youngest was patting a big bay which they had just bought from Miss Peel.

Miss Peel runs the local riding school and dealing establishment. She is small and wiry and one of those ageless people who might be thirty, or forty, or even fifty. She is a very good instructor and works from dawn to dark without ever seeming to make much money. She taught me most of what I know about riding.

Now Sonia was trying to mount the bay, and he was twirling all ways and banging her behind with his head. Tom, who dislikes the Stanmores, said,

"Look at her. Can't even mount her horse," and laughed scornfully.

The Stanmores' groom stepped forward then and held the bay. At the same moment I saw Guy Maunder arrive with his car and trailer.

Guy is dark with brown eyes. He was eighteen then and on leave from his National Service. He is the only son of the local M.P. I've known him since we both started riding at Miss Peel's and I had a pash on him when I was twelve. I still found him attractive and sometimes I would imagine us dining by candle light or spending a long dreamy day together on the river. But probably, because I admired him and because he was very popular in the neighbourhood, I never really expected it to happen.

Now he saw me and called, "Hullo, Jan. New horse?"

I said, "Miss Presscott's Velveteen. I'm schooling him."

And he said, "Is he nice?" while he unboxed his dark brown mare, Prudence.

A crowd of children had arrived by this time. The Stanmores were walking their horses up and down. The sleet had stopped falling. Velveteen was excited by the other horses and every few moments he let fly at one of them, so that I had to go away by myself and ride round and round an empty piece of road. I knew some of the foot followers and Angela, a school friend, came across and said, "Haven't you a mac? The forecast says snow."

"I've left it at home. I'm not staying out long," I answered.

I could see Sonia's bay running backwards into the pack. Tom cried, "Careful there, miss. Mind my hounds." Someone shooed the bay and Angela said, "She can't manage him, can she? Do you think she'll be all right?"

I didn't want to worry about Sonia, who was no friend of mine.

"I expect so," I replied, thinking, why have they put the horse in a twisted snaffle and running martingale? Everyone knew Miss Peel rode all her horses in plain or rubber snaffles and the bay was only young. I thought, they're asking for trouble.

Captain Williams arrived on his liver chestnut and Tom blew a short toot on his horn, before we moved off towards a copse in the fields by the river.

There were twenty or more of us by this time. I brought up the rear on Velveteen, who was still inclined to kick. It was bleaker than ever by the river. Guy was talking to the Stanmore girls. Tom put hounds into the copse and three or four rabbits scuttled away in front of us.

"There are still some left then," Captain Williams said. Presently Sonia began to have further trouble with the bay. He ran backwards, gave half rears and generally made a nuisance of himself. Then the first hound spoke, and he stood straight up on his hind legs and pawed the air. Sonia gave a little scream and at the same moment another hound spoke. Guy yelled, "Give him his head, Sonia or he'll topple over," and the bay wavered and came down with Sonia's arms round his neck and her heels clutching his sides. It was all over in a minute, but I think it left most of us shaking.

"Gosh, that was a near thing," said Chris who had just appeared on his grey mare. "If she's not careful she'll come a cropper before the day's over."

And now everyone was talking about the bay. "He's no girl's horse," Captain Williams said.

"No wonder Miss Peel sold him," exclaimed Guy. "I'm afraid you've been done this time, Sonia."

"He was all right when we tried him," drawled Audrey, who was still at one of the largest and smartest girls' public schools though she was nearly eighteen. "He went like a peach. He can't have been hunted before."

I didn't want to be drawn into an argument, but I'm fond of Miss Peel and I wasn't going to *let the cock crow thrice*.

"It's because you've put him into a twisted snaffle," I said, trying not to sound angry. "He's only young and it's awfully severe for him, and he *has* been hunted before and he behaved beautifully."

I thought, I sound a know-all and Guy will hate me and then there was a glorious burst of music and Tom was blowing the gone away; I forgot everything but the cry of hounds; the wind, the feel of Velveteen's rollicking stride and the fields which lay in front of us.

There was a scramble at a gate and a slippery slithery bank which led us into a lane sheltered by tall hedges; there was flying mud and foot followers who stood back as we galloped past, and little boys on bicycles and a couple of dachshunds on a lead. Then we were through another gate and galloping across damp river fields; and Velveteen's ears were forward, the other horses forgotten, his only interest the cry of hounds and the excitement of the chase. We came to a wire fence, which someone cut, and then to an osier bed with a ride down the centre and branches which slashed our faces. There was a smell of damp earth and stagnant streams before we were in the open again, galloping towards a cut and laid hedge. Hounds were close together and just behind them were Tom and his whip, Bruce. Above the sky was grey and behind us the wind whistled and howled across the open fields.

"This is fun," cried Chris, who enjoys every-thing and is the most uninhibited person I've ever met. "One needs a run on a day like this. It's perishing cold, but I love it, don't you?" I said, "The cold or the run?" But the wind drowned my voice and Chris galloped on in silence, his bowler rammed over his ears, his cheeks glowing and a smile of pure happiness on his round, cheerful face.

Velveteen hesitated and then jumped so that I pitched forward as he landed and lost a stirrup. Further along Sonia's bay took the hedge in his stride. And now hounds were swinging left towards a farmyard where cattle huddled by a fence and a tractor stood forlorn. Across the fields came the penetrating sickly sweet smell of silage, and Guy said, "That will stop them."

"You mean the silage?" asked Chris.

And Sonia said, "I hope they don't check. Benedictine's just settling down. Honestly I was terrified when he reared."

"I'm not surprised," Guy answered, sounding sympathetic and smiling at her with kind brown eyes. "It was a beastly rear."

Velveteen was blowing rather and I remember thinking, I'll have to take him home soon, and hating the thought.

Then, to everyone's surprise, hounds ran straight through the farmyard, across the main road and into the acres of plough beyond.

A man stood in the yard waving his cap. A dog pulled frantically at his chain and barked in an ecstasy of excitement. The road was wet and grey and very bleak. "He's a big dog fox," the man yelled.

"All right, mate," we heard Tom reply.

There was traffic halted on the road as we galloped through the yard—people standing on their running boards, craning out of windows, waving and the smell of petrol, the stench of oil, and after that wet plough and the first of the rain on our faces, and in the distance a beech wood, and a little hill topped by tall pines.

Velveteen made heavy weather of the plough. One after another the field swept past us.

"Hard luck!" cried Chris.

I hoped hounds would check at the wood, but they didn't, and now as I let Velveteen jog wearily across the plough I could hear Tom cheering them on, and a holloa from the far side, which made my blood run faster, and then the crash of music as hounds burst into the open again.

I should have turned for home then, but I didn't. I thought, it will do Velveteen good to follow quietly for a little while; and when I came to the end of the plough, I pushed him into a canter and rain dripped on us from the trees, which were bare and stood like sentinels in the wood, and there were the marks of many hoofs and the ground was squelchy under us.

We came to the open again and I nearly cheered; for there barely a hundred yards away was the field standing alongside a patch of kale. My spirits rose. I waved to Chris and he called: "Lucky for you," and I heard him laugh.

Guy turned in his saddle and looked at us. Then I saw that Sonia was having trouble with her bay again. His ears were back and he was ready to go backwards rather than forwards. I'm not an expert but I've ridden a great many different horses and I know all the danger signals, and one glance told me that Benedictine was going to rear the moment Sonia used her legs. Sonia's face was very white under her bowler. Her hands were clenched tightly on the reins and she looked terrified. I'd better tell her to turn him round if he starts to go up I thought, and Chris's eyes followed mine and he said,

"She's scared stiff, isn't she?"

"So am I. I feel something awful's going to happen," I replied, and it was true. For whatever Benedictine was like when Miss Peel sold him, he was no horse for Sonia now; sooner or later there would be a battle and he would come out top, and what would happen to Sonia one didn't know.

But the hounds were speaking again now. And everyone saw the big dog fox which came out of the kale and loped away across the bare fields towards a line of hills. I don't know how many people hollered, but I know Guy's was the finest of them all.

And then suddenly, as the field began to gallop,

and Tom blew the gone away and hounds came out of the kale with a glorious burst of music, the bay reared again. I noticed Sonia's white face and a lock of red hair which had escaped her net and lay across her forehead; and then, frightened beyond words I watched the bay paw the air with his forelegs. I saw him quiver and wanted to call, "Lean forward. Give him his head," but no words came. I thought, he'll come back to earth in a moment, God make him come down safely. But he didn't. He stayed up there for another split second and I watched Sonia slip back in her saddle and pull his mouth, and although she meant nothing to me I was paralysed with fear. I saw his hind legs quiver and at last words came and I called, "Put your arms round his neck. Drop the reins."

But it was too late. The horse's hind legs shook, he rocked and then very slowly he toppled over backwards.

Only a hundred yards away Tom was still blowing the gone away. The cry of hounds still rang merrily across the fields. I dismounted quickly and found that my knees were knocking. Sonia lay in a crumpled heap. The bay clambered to his feet as I approached. He looked shaken and was dripping with sweat. I thought, why does this have to happen to me? I shall have to get an ambulance. Suppose she's suffering from internal injuries? I'd better not move her—just put my coat over her. My hands were shaking too, and I thought, pull yourself together Jan, this isn't the way to behave in the face of an accident. And then I saw someone coming back across the fields and it was Guy.

2

"Gosh, how awful. I was afraid that something dreadful was going to happen, weren't you?" Guy asked, dismounting, glancing swiftly at Sonia.

"We'll need an ambulance, some tea in case she comes round and a blanket," I said. There didn't seem much time to waste. I took off my coat and Guy said, "Here have mine."

And I said, "She'd better have them both."

I held the three horses while I looked at Sonia, who lay still where she had fallen. Her hands looked limp and lifeless in their yellow gloves, and there was a nasty scratch across one side of her face. Her nose was rapidly turning blue.

"He must have caught her on the face with his

hoof," I said, putting our coats over Sonia, wondering what next? Where will there be a telephone? Looking for help in the bleak fields and seeing none.

"It's starting to rain," Guy said.

"We'll have to find a telephone," I told him.

"l know. I'll go. You stay here. I won't be long," Guy replied, handing me Benedictine and Velveteen, already mounting Prudence.

"Remember the tea and a blanket. It may be ages before the ambulance gets here," I said.

"Okay. Don't worry. I'll soon be back," he replied. "And don't try and move her."

"I wouldn't dream of it," I answered, watching him ride away, thinking why doesn't someone else come back?

Gradually, the cry of hounds grew fainter and every moment the rain fell more heavily, until I was standing with the two horses in a deluge, which soon soaked through my jersey and left me shivering with cold.

Now it was very quiet by the kale except for the sound of falling rain and the occasional jingle of bits when the horses banged their heads against one other. And I thought, I hope he hurries; Sonia will get pneumonia or pleurisy if she lies here for long in the rain. And I imagined Guy knocking on a door, smiling at someone with his expressive brown eyes, saying, "Please have you a telephone? There's been an accident."

He'll go into a room, I thought, and there'll be a fire and perhaps a dog, and he'll telephone for an ambulance and then at last he'll come back with a thermos of tea and a blanket; presently an ambulance will come and two men will put Sonia on a stretcher, very carefully so as not to hurt her injuries, and our nightmare will be over, or rather the worst of it will be.

But in the meantime Sonia still lay in the rain and there was nothing I could do. Occasionally she quivered and once she brushed a hand across her face and I thought at least she can move, that at least is something.

The morning and the meet at Little Cross all seemed to have happened a long time ago, and I wondered where the other Stanmores were now and whether they would come back and look for their sister.

Now the horses started to shiver and I thought, supposing Velveteen gets pneumonia? And saw myself ringing up Miss Presscott and trying to explain about the accident.

And then at last I saw Guy coming back and I saw that he had a blanket slung across Prudence's shoulder and a thermos in one hand. I waved and he put one thumb up and I knew that meant he had found an ambulance. My hopes rose then, and I thought perhaps she isn't hurt too badly after all. And I saw Guy and myself riding home in the rain.

"I've got some tea," he called as he came nearer, "and the ambulance shouldn't be long."

"She hasn't come round yet," I told him.

"The rain's a damned nuisance," he said, looking at the sky. "It looks as though it will keep on for hours. Does it mean she's badly hurt if she doesn't come round?" he asked a moment later.

"I don't know. My first aid doesn't go as far as that," I answered, and I thought, supposing she does? Do we let her sit up or tell her to stay where she is?

"If she doesn't come round soon we may as well have some of the tea. I brought a big thermos," Guy said.

"Where did you go?" I asked.

"To a house with diamond panes and an Alsatian. The people were splendid," he said.

I glanced at Sonia and, as I looked, she seemed to move and I thought, I hope the ambulance comes soon.

"She looks all in, doesn't she? Hadn't we better walk the horses up and down?" Guy asked.

We put the blanket over Sonia and for a moment her eyes opened and I saw that they were grey.

"Poor girl," murmured Guy, "I hope she's all right."

We walked the horses backwards and forwards across the field and the rain soaked through my gloves until my hands were numb, and Guy's hunting shirt clung to his back as though glued. And gradually twilight seemed to come and Guy said, "They told me they wouldn't delay. I've just realised that I should have rung up Tumbling Fields."

"Perhaps someone else has had an accident," I suggested.

"They hadn't when I rang up."

Tumbling Fields is the Stanmores' house; it is large and barrack-like and looks across fields, which are full of kingcups in the summer, to the river.

They have a meet of hounds there every season. Mr. Stanmore is a business man and very wealthy. Mrs. is small and gay and hunts sometimes on an ancient roan called Robin. The daughters are very like their father.

"We might as well have some tea," said Guy. "I've no idea when the ambulance will be here now."

I watched him pour out the tea. A crash cap suited his well-defined features. I saw that there was mud on his nose. "Here you are," he said, turning round suddenly and catching my eyes on his face. "I forgot to get any sugar so, if you like it, I'm afraid you'll have to do without."

"I don't so it's okay. Thanks very much," I replied, taking the thermos top from him filled with steaming tea.

"I'm sorry I couldn't lace it with rum for you. Unfortunately I don't carry a flask," he said.

He sounded serious so I said, "It's lovely how it is, thank you," and as the hot liquid ran down my throat, I felt warmth come back into my body.

I handed back the thermos top when it was empty and took off my gloves and put my hands, which were aching now they had thawed, into my pocket, and felt like whistling until I remembered Sonia lying in the wind and the rain. The horses had stopped shivering. Their tack looked wet and grey and slimy.

"Gosh, what a day," I said, glancing at the dark stormy sky which promised nothing but more rain. And soon it will be dark, I thought, because on wet days it comes soon, and there will be the ride home together after the ambulance comes, and later I shall ring up the hospital and find how Sonia is.

And then we saw the ambulance coming towards us across the squelchy field, and Guy screwed up his forehead and looked at it, and said, "At last. About time too."

He looked very wet and cold. He had taken off his cap and his dark hair lay plastered against his head. I noticed how tall he was. When you're tall yourself you find you look at men and think I could dance with him. Looking at Guy I knew my chin would just reach his shoulder. I wondered whether he could dance and then remembered Sonia and thought how heartless I was and said, "How long do you think it will take to get her into hospital?"

"I don't know," Guy answered, signalling to the ambulance, calling, "Over here. More to your right," through the wind and the rain and the early twilight.

It arrived at last. Two men jumped out in uniform and apologised, "We're sorry we've been so long, sir. We couldn't find you."

"It's all right, she's over there," Guy said.

For an awful moment, I thought supposing she's dead? She looked so limp and crumpled lying still beneath the coats. I think Guy felt the same. I remember he too seemed suddenly scared. He felt in his pockets and produced cigarettes for the first time that disastrous day. And though I had only smoked once before, I took one because suddenly I needed something to take my mind off Sonia, who looked so ghastly as the men took off the blanket and the coats. Guy lit my cigarette. I saw that his hand was trembling; he looked at it and said, "Silly. Pure nerves."

They started to put Sonia on the stretcher, and Guy called, "Anything we can do?"

"You can have your coats back, I should think you're wet to the skin," one of them said.

We collected our coats, but they weren't much use, because the rain had soaked through to the linings by this time.

"Hell," said Guy, and, "I'm freezing, aren't you?"

"Yes."

They were putting Sonia into the ambulance now. Inside the light was on.

"We may as well go," Guy said.

They shut the doors. We mounted our horses. "Shall I lead the bay?" asked Guy.

One of the men was inside the ambulance with Sonia. The other came across to us with the blanket.

He had lit a cigarette too. "We won't need this. I don't think there's anything broken. But of course we don't know what may have happened inside. You say the horse rolled on her?" he asked.

"No, toppled over—fell over backwards. Actually I didn't see it, but Jan did," Guy replied looking at me.

The man produced a pad and pencil.

"I'll just trouble you for her address; then we'll be off," he said.

"Miss Sonia Stanmore, Tumbling Fields, Beckley 6," Guy recited.

We rode away as the engine started and, for a moment, the wheels spun round.

"Oh dear, they're going to stick," Guy said. But they didn't; very slowly the ambulance bumped and slid away across the field until we couldn't see it any more.

"I suppose we'd better go to Miss Peel's first, hadn't we?" Guy asked.

We came to the house with the diamond panes and the Alsatian. There was crazy paving leading to the front door, a lily pond by the gate.

"Shall I go?" asked Guy.

"Well, you know the people," I said.

He took the thermos and the blanket and gave me the horses to hold.

At last the rain was stopping. We had crossed Benedict's stirrups over the top of his saddle. He seemed subdued, as though he sensed that somehow he had caused a tragedy.

Guy came back and we rode on along a bleak road where the rain lay in puddles and ran blithely into gutters cut in the grass verges. The sky cleared. Somewhere a bird sang.

"Poor Sonia. It's awful isn't it?" Guy asked.

"Awful," I agreed, and wondered whether they cared a lot for each other, whether they danced together and dined by candle light. Then I thought again how heartless I was, and how Sonia might be ill for months or even die, while I could still walk and ride and talk. I suppose I was tired, or suffering from some sort of shock, because suddenly I felt like bursting into tears. I blew my nose and we rode on in silence until Guy saw a telephone kiosk.

"At last. I'd better ring up the Stanmores," he exclaimed then, as though it had been on his mind for hours.

Again I held the horses, and now the cars that passed had lights which shone round the corners before they came and when they had gone left the road darker than before.

It was a long time before Guy returned from the kiosk. The horses were fretting by then and twilight was darkening into dusk.

"Mrs. Stanmore was very upset, but she took it splendidly. The other girls aren't back yet. Apparently they've already bought the horse, so it's no good leaving him at Miss Peel's. They're sending Small to meet us," Guy told me.

Small was the Stanmores' groom and a man I had never liked. He had dark shifty eyes and a hint of an Irish accent. He had taught the girls to ride, and what he said went in their stables.

"So now, *Home James and don't spare the horses*," quoted Guy, mounting, with a grin, taking Benedictine, pushing Prudence into a trot.

Home, I thought, a ride home together in the gathering dusk. There were lots of things I wanted to say to Guy, but suddenly I felt shy. He looked remote too and very aloof as we trotted on along the shadowy country road. He sat a horse with a certain dash which made one think of cavaliers and of Carrying the *Good News from Ghent to Aix*. He rode very well in a happy slapdash way, which seemed to make Prudence feel happy too.

I wanted to ask him to come to tea one day and to find out whether he would be coming to the Hunt Ball. And then I remembered how shabby our house was inside and how he was used to Littlewick Court and heaps of servants. And I thought, if I ask him about the Hunt Ball he'll think I'm looking for an escort. So in the end I said nothing and we trotted on and on in the same endless silence.

It was quite dark by the time we reached Little Cross and I think we both jumped when Small called, "I'm 'ere, sir."

"Oh hullo," called Guy. "I couldn't think who it was."

"I'm ever so sorry to hear about Miss Sonia," Small said.

"Yes, it was rotten luck. Have they heard anything from the hospital yet?" Guy asked.

"Not that I knows of. Good evening, Miss," Small replied, catching sight of me.

We had drawn rein. Now Small took Benedictine.

"I always said he was no good," he told us

looking at the bay. "Why Madam wanted to buy him I can't see. Not as though he's much to look at either."

I wanted to stick up for Benedictine. I felt sorry for him returning to the Stanmores' stable in disgrace. I couldn't help feeling that what had happened wasn't entirely his fault.

But Guy said, "It's a pity," and the moment was past.

"Good night then," Small called, taking another road. We could hear him shouting at Benedictine as he disappeared into the darkness, and gradually the sound of the bay's hoofs grew fainter until it disappeared altogether.

"I don't know why we're standing here. You look wet to the skin," Guy said.

We rode on together through the damp and the dark. We talked about hospitals and whether Sonia would remember anything when she came round. We recollected the days we had spent at the riding school, and which ponies we had liked and which had stuck at the gate, making us feel fools. We came to cross-roads and Guy said,

"Would you like me to see you home?"

"It's all right, thank you very much. Prudence must be tired, don't bother," I replied.

We said goodnight to one another; and then we were riding away from one another towards our separate homes, and I began to think of Sonia again lying in hospital and to wonder whether her sisters were still looking for her.

It wasn't far to our house. When I reached the yard, Daddy was filling up buckets and all the lights were on. He heard Velveteen's hoofs coming along the road and called, "Is that you Jan? We were afraid something had happened to you."

I realised then that I should have telephoned my parents.

"It wasn't me. It was Sonia Stanmore. She had to have an ambulance. I'm sorry I didn't ring up," I called back, riding into the yard, dismounting, finding that my legs were stiff and my whole body ached from being so long in wet clothes.

"I'm so sorry. Have you had an awful day?" Mummy called from the kitchen.

I settled the horses for the night and related the events of the day to my parents. I had a glorious hot bath and a boiled egg and thick slices of bread and butter and cup after cup of tea. Then I rang up the Stanmores. Audrey answered.

"Hullo, who's there?" she asked.

"It's Jan, Jan Craigson. I rang up to inquire after Sonia. Do you know how she is yet?" I asked.

"Mummy's with her now. She's come round. They think she's only suffering from concussion," Audrey replied.

I thought, is that all? and felt suddenly immensely relieved.

"They don't think there are any internal injuries?" I asked.

"No, nothing except concussion," Audrey repeated, and I thought she might thank me for my trouble. But she didn't. She said, "There's the dinner gong. Goodbye."

I called, "I'm so glad it's only concussion." But she had hung up. Somehow I felt squashed as I replaced the receiver and switched off the hall light. She might have said, did you get back all right or something, I thought. Anyway it's all over now. I can forget the whole incident, Guy included, I decided, turning to go into the sitting room. But the silly thing was, it wasn't—everything was just beginning.

3
————

THE next day was Sunday. I wakened to find that I was stiff all over; I remembered riding home with Guy. Outside it was just getting light. I thought, Sunday, a lovely lazy day, and fell asleep again to dream that Guy and I were dancing together in a room overlooking a sandy shore. It was summer and the room was full of flowers. We were the only dancers and my frock was blue and silver. Much later I heard Daddy making tea in the kitchen. I heard him drop the kettle and then I got out of bed and dressing quickly went downstairs.

"Just in time," Daddy said, meeting me with a cup of tea in his hand. Except for Sundays it is generally me who makes the early morning tea; now I said, "Thank you. Did the kettle fall on your foot?"

It was just like any other Sunday; there was

nothing to tell me that there would be all sorts of surprises before nightfall.

When I visited the stables Velveteen was looking dreamy as horses do after hunting. Domino wasn't clipped so I turned him out in the paddock.

I had finished the stables by nine and we all had breakfast together on the big table in the kitchen. Usually breakfast is a scrappy meal in our house. The coffee pot stays hot on the Rayburn cooker and we all help ourselves to what we want when we want it. But on Sundays we always have boiled eggs and lots of toast in the silver toast rack, and the marmalade is in its proper dish, and there's a feeling of leisure about the meal and a paper for each of us to read. I always look at my horoscope and I had just found the right page when the telephone rang.

I said, "Shall I answer?"

And Mummy said, "Yes, it's probably for you."

Daddy was reading about a scandalous murder in Notting Hill Gate. I don't think he even heard the telephone. Anyway, he just went on reading.

I picked up the receiver and a voice which I recognised as Miss Peel's said, "Hullo, is that Jan?"

She sounded anxious, as though she had had a nasty surprise and had still to get over it.

"Yes, hullo Miss Peel," I answered, and imagined her telephoning from her saddle room, which is full of rosettes and photographs as well as tack.

"Jan, I wonder if you can help me. Something awful happened." I thought, she's going to tell me about Sonia.

I said, "You mean the accident. I was there."

"Oh were you? You know all about it then," she said. "It wasn't all Benedictine's fault was it? I can't believe it. You know I broke him myself and he's always been the sweetest horse imaginable."

I remembered how I had hoped to forget yesterday. It didn't seem as though I was to be allowed to.

"Well, he did rear," I said. "But you know they put him in a twisted snaffle and running martingale, and I don't think he liked it much."

I remembered Benedictine standing on his hind legs and the awful terrifying moments before he toppled over. It was something I wanted to forget. No one who rides likes to remember accidents and the same thing might happen to me one day.

"Everyone's saying terrible things about him. They say I sold the Stanmores a rogue," said Miss Peel and there was a tremble in her voice as she spoke. Suddenly she sounded old, and I remembered how proud she had always been of her reputation.

I said, "I'm terribly sorry." I wondered why she had rung me up. Outside the sky was almost blue. The rain had completely disappeared.

"They say he's good for nothing but horse meat,"

she continued.

"Well, that's absolute rot," I said. I wanted to get back to breakfast and to finish reading my horoscope. "I'm terribly sorry," I repeated.

I thought, I'll say goodbye in a moment. Then I remembered how fond one becomes of horses and I was immensely sorry for Miss Peel. "Is there anything I can do? I'll contradict any wrong rumours of course," I said.

Miss Peel seemed to sigh a great sigh of relief. "Yes, you can help," she told me. "You know I've broken my collar bone."

I didn't. I said, "I'm so sorry."

"Well it doesn't matter anyway. The point is I can't do anything about Benedictine. And they're going to have him destroyed or send him to a sale without a warranty. They aren't even going to give him a second chance," she said. "The silly thing is I never wanted them to have him. They've been taught by that awful man Small and they're quite incapable of riding a young horse, Sonia most of all."

She wants me to have him, I thought now, oh damn, damn, damn. I didn't want another horse in my stable and certainly not Benedictine who would probably cause nothing but trouble.

"But they insisted," she continued. And I could see Mrs. Stanmore with her firm chin and Sonia with her obstinate mouth, determined that they would have Benedictine at any cost; and now they'll be equally determined that he's useless, I thought.

"And so in the end I let them take him, and now this has happened," she said with a choke in her voice.

I suddenly felt very angry. I didn't want Benedictine. I wanted to forget the whole thing. It was nothing to do with me. And yet I was fond of Miss Peel and I thought the horse should have a second chance ... I was in a hopeless situation.

"So I just wondered if you could have him just for a few days, just to show everyone he *is* all right," Miss Peel finished.

I wanted time to think. "Can I ring you back?" I asked.

"Oh dear. It's all so difficult. It's really a matter of life and death. The woman who lives next door knows Small and everything's to be settled today," she said.

Outside the sun was shining. It was a day for falling in love, for making new plans, for starting again. It was more like April than December. I remembered Miss Peel giving me my first riding lesson on a little Dartmoor pony called Rex; riding in my first show, and Miss Peel consoling me when I came out first in the musical chairs. I remembered running down to the riding school before breakfast, staying all day, coming home tired and happy in the gathering dusk.

I thought, Domino's going on Wednesday, and there's a box free.

I said, "Yes, all right. I'll do what I can."

"Bless you Jan. I know he'll be all right with you," she said.

"I don't know about that. He was standing up all over the place yesterday," I replied.

But Miss Peel was determined that there was nothing wrong with Benedictine. It was all Sonia's fault and I was to prove it.

She said, "Do you think you can get to Tumbling Fields quite soon? I don't think there's much time to waste."

"Yes, just as soon as I can," I answered.

"I'll pay you of course," she said.

I didn't want to be paid. My debts to Miss Peel would never be paid. She had made poetry of my youth, taught me how to ride; whatever I could do now would be small return for that.

I said, "Don't let's talk about it now."

"Bless you," she replied and hung up.

I stood in the hall and thought, I'd better take my bicycle and that there wouldn't be time to change if it was really a matter of life and death. I wondered what I would say to the Stanmores. Then I went back into the kitchen.

Daddy had changed his paper. He was reading *Runaway Horse Injures Two*. Mummy was pouring herself a second of coffee. I wasn't interested in breakfast now. I said, "Miss Peel wants me to have Benedictine. I've agreed. I hope you don't mind." But I knew they would. They would worry each time I rode the bay; imagine accidents; I almost wished I had refused to have the horse as I waited to say something. The clock on the chimneypiece seemed to tick away into eternity. Daddy put down his paper. Mummy said, "Oh, Jan."

"It's really quite all right. Miss Peel broke him herself. It's just that he and Sonia don't get on together," I told them. Daddy had taken off the spectacles he wears for reading.

"Won't it be rather a lot for you to look after?" he asked.

"Domino's going on Wednesday. I couldn't very well refuse. Miss Peel's broken her collar bone and can't have him back," I explained.

"Well, do be careful," Mummy said. "Jump off if you feel him going up."

"And if he gets too much for you, send him back to Miss Peel, broken collar bone or not," Daddy told me.

They didn't understand the situation; but there wasn't time to explain. I had to get to the Stanmores' as quickly as I could. The day didn't seem like

Sunday any more. I ran upstairs for my riding jacket. I was wearing jeans, old shoes and a checked American style shirt. There was straw in my hair and I hadn't made up my face at all, but I remembered that I was to hurry. So I combed out the straw, put on my jacket and then ran downstairs and out to the shed where my bicycle lives. The morning was still lovely; there were birds singing and the sun cast long shadows across the yard.

Tumbling Fields is about three and a half miles from our house. As I pedalled I wondered once again what I would say to the Stanmores. They wouldn't like me turning up and expecting to take Benedictine home. I'm not a particularly good rider, often I fall off when other people wouldn't and I've never been higher than third in a dressage test. What successes I've had with horses has always been due to a psychological approach.

I put myself in the horse's place, try to discover his past history and after a lot of thought I generally discover why he is misbehaving. Very often, of course, it is only the result of too many oats and too little work, or just plain bad riding, but sometimes one can trace the trouble back to a misunderstanding, or an accident, or wrong bitting, or sometimes it's just too tight a brow band or a saddle which pinches. At the time of writing, people were beginning to send me horses labelled difficult, impossible and occasionally vicious. Following the assumption that most of those sorts of horses are usually both clever and highly strung, I had so far been extremely lucky in my cures.

But I didn't expect the Stanmores to know anything about the reputation I was laboriously creating for myself. To them I was just a girl who mucked about with horses and generally had straw in her hair. I belonged to the nebulous gang of people they labelled *horsy*. They took it for granted that I wasn't interested in anything else and were careful not to invite me to their parties. I knew that they imagined that I talked and thought of nothing but horse. That I had helped to rescue Sonia would have done nothing to alter that impression.

I thought of all this as I pedalled my bicycle towards Tumbling Fields. I was filled with misgiving. I could only hope that Miss Peel had already telephoned them. I took the back drive which I knew led to the stables. I wished now that I had made up my face. Lipstick would have heightened my morale, as it was I felt more and more disreputable and boringly horsy the nearer I drew to the yard and my encounter with the Stanmores.

What was I going to say? How would I greet them? I hadn't decided anything. And now I had reached the yard and could see horses looking over loose box doors and Small polishing a pair of stirrups in the saddle room. I must admit I almost turned back then. I thought, supposing I do ride him and fall off in front of them all? And I dismounted from my bicycle with shaky legs and not for the first time wished that I had never set eyes on Benedictine. Small waved from the saddle room.

"Morning, Miss," he called.

I waved back. I propped my bicycle against the wall, blew my nose and then I couldn't put the moment off any longer.

"Do you know whether Audrey and Susan are in please?" I asked, and ran my hands through my hair as I spoke and found another piece of straw.

"They're in the house I think, Miss," he said. "Would you like me to get them on the phone?"

I saw a field telephone then on a little table in the saddle room. I thought it like the Stanmores to have the house and stables connected by phone. Somehow it made them less horsy; they didn't have to be always down at the stables. As you can see I was disliking them more each moment.

"Yes, please," I said.

I don't know who answered. But very soon Small was saying, "Will you tell Miss Audrey and Miss Susan that Miss Craigson's here to see them."

He put back the receiver and said, "They'll be here shortly," and then, "Well, how are you this morning? Not suffering any ill effects after your soaking yesterday I hope."

"No, I'm fine thank you," I answered, and saw three figures approaching and saw with horror that one was Guy. My heart seemed to leap and then beat much faster than usual. He was wearing a herringbone suit. The girls were dressed in skirts and jumpers; round Audrey's neck there was a single string of pearls.

I looked at my jeans with increased dislike.

"Hullo Jan," Guy called.

I called back, "Hullo." I thought, don't be silly, Jan, clothes don't matter. Anyway even if you like Guy, there's no reason to suppose that he likes you. But it didn't make any difference. I felt shy and awkward and just what the Stanmores thought I was —horsy. And the reason for my call didn't make things any better. When they reached me, I said, "How's Sonia?"

"Marvellous. She's coming home this afternoon," Audrey replied.

"I think she was jolly lucky being rescued by Guy," said Susan. "I think I shall come to grief next time we hunt."

"Jan was there too. She did nearly everything," Guy said, smiling at me.

"Did you get back all right?" I asked him, because I felt I must say something.

"Yes, just in time for a belated tea," he said.

And now a silence fell and I knew I had to explain the reason for my visit.

"Miss Peel asked me to come. She wants me to ride Benedictine—just to show he's really all right," I said.

It sounded horribly conceited, as though I thought I was a wonderful rider but what else was I to say? They all looked surprised—Guy most of all.

I wanted to say, "I don't think I can ride better than any of you. I'm just doing it for Miss Peel." But the words wouldn't come.

Guy was looking at me as though I was the most extraordinary person. A lump was rising in my throat. I wanted him to like me. I wanted to explain just how everything had happened, that I wasn't just horsy, that I liked him more than Chris, more than any of the other boys I had ever met. But I couldn't. I was tongue tied. And anyway how could I explain it all in a stableyard in front of Small, Audrey and Susan? For Small was there too listening to every word and looking just as surprised as the rest.

"I see. Well, of course you can, if you're sure you want to. We can't be responsible for what happens though," said Audrey.

"You must be mad. He was awful yesterday after you left. Wasn't he, Small?" asked Susan.

"He certainly was. I wouldn't ride him if I were

you, Miss," Small said.

I had the feeling that Small had never liked the horse. Hadn't he said, "I can't see why Madam ever bought him?"

"Well, I promised Miss Peel I would, and I don't want to let her down," I answered.

"I think you're awfully brave," Guy said. Small went to fetch some tack and I called after him, "I'll have a rubber snaffle if you've got one and no martingale please."

I felt horribly nervous but all the same the worst seemed past—at least the Stanmores knew why I had come.

"We were just off to church," Susan said.

"Well, don't let me put you off going," I replied, hoping that they would go and leave me to ride Benedictine alone.

"We wouldn't dream of it now," said Audrey.

And I thought, they are hoping to pick up the bits.

I hadn't realised how tall Benedictine was until I came to mount him. I let down the stirrup, Small held his head and the others just stood and watched. But once in the saddle, my fears vanished. I felt immensely safe; the feel of the reins between my fingers, and the stirrups on my feet were marvellously familiar. I felt that nothing could scare me now.

"Mind he doesn't go up," said Guy looking down at the cobbled yard.

I forgot everyone but Benedictine as I rode across the yard to the little paddock behind the stables. I felt him hesitate as we approached the gate. I spoke to him and he went on. I could feel what he was thinking—I had only to anticipate his thoughts and I would be safe. Once he tried to rear and I swung him round in a half circle and then pushed him into a canter. Gradually as he realised that the snaffle was plain and my legs were just behind the girth, he settled down and went like a dream, and I realised with a start just why Miss Peel was so anxious that he should not be destroyed. He was a horse in a thousand; his stride was long and low; he had great depth of girth, a beautiful shoulder. He might not be a show horse, but he had tremendous possibilities.

Presently Guy called, "Jolly good."

And Audrey said, "It's all very well. You wait till he's in the hunting field, he'll do exactly the same thing again."

I said, "I bet he doesn't."

She replied, "I bet he does."

I said, "How much?"

"If you're really going to lay stakes, don't you think you'd better let me be the bookie?" suggested Guy.

"A pound," said Audrey.

"Okay," I agreed.

Both the Stanmore girls were looking furious now.

"Can I take him home with me?" I asked.

"I don't see why not," Audrey replied.

"Hadn't we better ask Mummy?" asked Susan.

"I don't see why. She wanted to have him destroyed," Audrey said. "Why not let Jan have him if she thinks she can do something. I only hope he doesn't break her neck," she said, looking at me.

"I'll be hunting him next Saturday then," I said.

"You're mad," Guy told me.

"And if he rears I'm to give you a pound, whether I fall off or not. Okay?"

"Okay," agreed Audrey.

I turned and rode down the drive. I was filled with a sense of recklessness. If I had been wearing a hat I would have thrown it in the air. I began to sing as I rode towards home.

Church bells were ringing. Men were tinkering with cars, lighting bonfires, clearing their gardens. Everyone was thinking of spring, though it was December and the worst of the winter was yet to come.

It wasn't until I reached our house that I was suddenly filled with misgiving. What if I couldn't ride Benedictine after all? Supposing he stood up in the hunting field and I had to take him home? What a fool I would look. Though that didn't matter. It was Benedictine and Miss Peel who mattered.

Mummy met me in the yard. "I've just finished speaking to Mrs. Stanmore," she said. "She rang me up."

I thought what does that mean? She can't have Benedictine back now.

"She's upset about you having the horse; she says he's dangerous. She thought she ought to speak to me," Mummy said.

There was a funny feeling in the pit of my stomach. I didn't want to lose Benedictine; but I didn't want to hurt Mummy either.

"I said that it was up to you, that we trusted you absolutely. But you will be careful, Jan, won't you?"

If I had been on the ground I would have kissed her then. I said, "Oh Mummy you are marvellous. Yes, I will be careful, honestly I will."

"It's your father, he worries so," she said.

I swore then that I wouldn't take any unnecessary risks. I put Benedictine in the empty box and fetched him hay and water. I stood and looked at his Roman nose and plain bay head. He was a horse who grew on me. When at last I went in to lunch he had become handsome in my eyes and a wonderful addition to my stable.

As I strained the brussels sprouts into the sink I thought, I've got five days, just five days.

4

I WAKENED next morning at six-thirty and, for a moment, I couldn't think why I felt so excited and so incredibly happy. Then I remembered Benedictine. I dressed quickly, rushed downstairs and out into the pitch darkness of the yard. I switched on the lights and there he was with his long Roman nose and his large eyes, plain and bay, a horse which I already loved.

Much later I schooled him in our field before hacking through the December sunshine, down the lanes where the trees and banks were bare, over windswept hilltops, and dreaming water meadows and then home as dusk came to the winter land-scape and cars switched on their lights, and men returned from work.

At first he was nervous, but gradually as he

realised that the snaffle was made of rubber, he settled and gave me a lovely ride.

I returned to find Chris standing in the yard, his bicycle propped against the stable wall.

"Gosh, you *have* been ages. I thought you were never coming," he said. "It's true then that you have got that beastly bay."

I ignored the insult. "Yes, he's mine for the time being. I'm hunting him on Saturday," I replied, dismounting, leading Benedictine to his box, wondering why Chris had called.

"You're potty," he said in his usual good-humoured way. "Absolutely nuts."

"I like the horse. He's one in a thousand," I replied. "I'm not surprised Miss Peel didn't relish the idea of him being destroyed."

"Well, I'll be out to pick you up on Saturday," Chris said.

I put Benedictine away. Chris helped me feed the other horses; then I suggested a cup of tea. We went indoors and found Mummy toasting crumpets. One of the nice things about Chris is the way he'll try his hand at anything; now he took the fork from Mummy and said, "Let me do it."

I never feel the house is shabby when Chris comes to tea. And if it was ten times shabbier I don't think he would care. But our friendship is strictly Platonic and I was surprised when he took the toasted crumpet off the fork and said, "I wondered whether you would come to the ball with me on Friday—that is if you're not already fixed up?"

The Hunt Ball had caused me a great deal of anguish. I had always meant to go. I had prayed that someone would ask me. Months ago Mummy and I had planned to make a dress for it, but no one had suggested that I went with them and I jibbed at asking any of the boys I knew, and the dress had never been made. I thought of all this before I saw Chris was blushing and probably imagining that I didn't want to go with him, while really I was only wondering what I could wear.

I said, "Yes, I'd love to. Thank you so much," and then, because everyone knows that Chris is still being educated, "But you must let me pay for my ticket."

"Don't be silly. It's on me. It's jolly nice of you to come at the last minute."

I guessed then that someone had let him down.

"I'll collect you in the car and we'll have dinner somewhere first," he said.

Chris is a wonderful companion. I told him all about accident as we had tea together, about riding Benedictine at the Stanmores, about the bet.

When I had finished, he said, "I think I'm rather glad I'm not you. But still, if it comes off, it certainly will be one in the eye for the Stanmores, and I see what you mean about Miss Peel."

I looked at him eating crumpets and honey and knew I had an ally. "You don't think I've been a fool?" I asked. "I mean if he does rear I shall lose a pound."

"No, I think you've taken a gamble, but I would back you any day against Sonia Stanmore," Chris said.

After we had washed up we played the gramophone and tried dancing together. I had been taught by Mummy; Chris had had a few lessons at a dancing school. At first we stumbled over each other's feet, but gradually we improved, until Chris stopped and, with his arm round my waist, said, "We'll be a show piece soon. You dance beautifully, Jan."

I thought of Guy then, of my dream, of us dancing together. Would he be there? Would he ask me? I said, "So do you," and thought, I must do something about my hair, buy some sandals. Suddenly I was determined to be ravishing, to surprise everyone and, most important of all, show the Stanmores that I wasn't just a horsy girl.

We danced for a little longer and then Chris said, "I must go, or I shall be late for supper."

I said, "Thanks for coming, it's been lovely."

"Thanks for the tea," he replied.

I watched him go and my mind was full of the

ball. He was to fetch me at seven-thirty. We would dine at eight. I had never been to a ball before. I waved as he turned into the road. I ran indoors. I looked at myself in the hall mirror, scraped back my hair, piled it on top of my head. Somehow I had to look different.

I found Mummy and said, "How shall I do my hair? I'm tired of it how it is. It's so ordinary."

We went upstairs and tried it all ways in the bathroom. I kept saying, "I don't want to look horsy. I mustn't look horsy."

Finally Mummy said, "Why don't you have the ends loosely permed? You've got such lovely hair it would be a shame to cut it off."

Supposing it looks awful afterwards, I thought. It'll be too late to do anything then.

Mummy seemed to read my thoughts, for she said, "The new cold perms are very good. It won't go fuzzy." We ploughed through a mass of magazines until we found a style we liked. Then I said, "What on earth shall I do about a dress? If only Chris had asked me before."

"Don't panic. There's lots of time still. We'll buy material tomorrow, find a pattern and I'll run it up for you," Mummy replied.

"You are an angel," I said, and thought, I'd like it to be blue and silver.

"I'll lend you my fur coat," Mummy offered.

We stayed up for hours that night making plans. Next morning was Tuesday. I rode Benedictine early. I rang the hairdresser at nine. Ten o'clock found Mummy and myself catching a bus into Summertown.

The weather had changed. It was very cold. The hedges and grass were hoary with frost. The east wind had returned. The sky looked like snow.

We shivered as we waited for the bus and I thought, I hope it isn't like this on Saturday.

Summertown was nearly empty. It was a long time before we found any suitable material. I was looking for blue and silver and Mummy was thinking of gold and black. In the end we compromised and bought a length of gold and red brocade. The red was darker than scarlet and not as deep as crimson.

"We'll have to find you gold sandals now," Mummy said.

"And an evening bag, and a pattern," I added.

By the time we had bought everything it was nearly one and I still had three horses to ride. We caught the next bus by the skin of our teeth, and now it was snowing in large flakes as though it would never stop.

I thought about Christmas as we travelled home, about the card I would buy Guy and what I would write inside.

"You'll need ear-rings," said Mummy as we reached the front door. "I've got a pair which will do."

I hadn't time for a proper lunch. We had omelettes and new bread and afterwards the meringues we had bought in Summertown.

I changed into riding clothes and rode Domino. It was even colder now and the snow was lying as though it meant to stay.

At three o'clock I changed on to Velveteen. It was dark when at last I mounted Fantasy, at least as dark as it ever is with snow. I rode her as fast as I dared and the snow balled in her feet and the wind slapped my face until it was numb and didn't seem to belong any more. And all the time I was thinking about the Hunt Ball, so that when she shied and swung round on her hocks, I stayed where I was.

I hit the ground with my shoulder and scrambling to my feet watched Fantasy gallop back the way we had come with dismay in my heart. I couldn't blame anyone but myself. She had come to me because she shied. But that didn't make things any better. My feet, which had been numb for some time, came back to life as I walked homewards. Someone leaned out of a lorry and called, "What's the matter? Lost your gee gee?"

I thought how awful it would be if she galloped back to her own home. I imagined her owner, a learned professor, ringing me up. What would he say? Or, more important, what would I say? And supposing she fell and broke her knees? I started to run then, with one eye on her hoof prints, not yet covered by snow.

I thought, bother the Hunt Ball. Why can't I stop thinking about it and Guy? I thought, you're going to pieces, Jan, and all over a boy who probably doesn't care a damn for you. I thought, you're not in love with him, so don't think you are. But nothing helped. As I ran along the snow covered road after one of my client's favourite horses, I could only think of Guy Maunder and what I would say to him at the Hunt Ball.

A car passed me with chains. A man opened a window and called, "Are you looking for a horse, Miss? One passed a few minutes back."

I shouted, "Thank you." And now the hoof marks were obliterated by snow, and my legs were aching and I was out of breath. I broke into a walk, and thought, don't fuss, Jan, she'll probably be waiting for you in the yard. I thought, I suppose men wear tails at balls and wondered whether there would be candlelight.

I started to run again, and the wind must have changed, because now the snow was in my eyes and nose and hair.

I put one hand in front of my eyes and blundered on.

I thought, if Guy's there, he'll probably be in a party, and then I thought, if she has hurt herself how shall I break it to the professor?

And now I was much too hot; my hands were throbbing in their gloves and there was a trickle of sweat running down my face.

I thought, you don't deserve to have people's horses to school, Jan Craigson. Any ordinary horseman would have stayed on that shy.

I took off my gloves and undid my coat. I pulled my crash cap further over my eyes. I tripped over the road where the surface changed, and now I could hardly see, the snow was falling so fast. And then suddenly I was home. And there was Fantasy standing in the yard looking sheepish, just as I had hoped. I felt a great wave of relief then. I thought, I needn't have fussed at all, and then I saw that she was bleeding and there was a gash on one of her hocks, and a lump rose in my throat and I thought, she can't be hurt, this can't have happened to me. But it had happened. The curtains were drawn in the kitchen; the snow and the wind had combined to obliterate the sound of her hoofs. Across the yard was a thin trickle of blood, very vivid against the whiteness of the snow.

I stood in a daze for a moment. I knew it was all

my own fault. I had no excuse to offer the professor. I wished at that moment that I had never met Guy, nor been invited to the Hunt Ball. Then I walked forward saying, "Poor little Fantasy. Whoa Fantasy." One of her reins was broken and my best saddle was terribly scratched on one side. But both her stirrups were there and she wasn't cut anywhere but on her hock and that didn't look too bad.

I put her back in her box and took off the tack and rugged her up. I hurried indoors and fetched water and antiseptic and a big wad of cotton wool.

I bathed her hock and decided she would need an anti-tetanus injection, and went indoors and rang up Bill Strawley, the vet.

There was a note on the kitchen table saying, *Gone for a drink. Be back soon.* I stood and looked at it and thought, what shall I say to the professor? And I can't go on like this. I've got to pull myself together. And then I thought, perhaps he won't speak to me at the ball and then I can stop thinking about him. I pulled back the curtains and looked at the snow still falling and thought, gosh, you're a fool, Jan.

I went outside and fed and watered the other horses and straightened the boxes. I'll just say Fantasy slipped in the snow, I decided, slipped and came down. After all it's true. I looked at her hock again and saw that it was swelling and thought, I'll have to keep her for nothing until she's recovered. And then I saw a car swing into the drive.

Mr. Strawley is young with a quiet voice, large capable hands and with the reputation of being the best vet within thirty miles of Summertown. Now he got out of his car and said, "What's the trouble?" When I had finished explaining, he looked at Fantasy and said, "She's not too bad. But she'll be lame for a little while I'm afraid. I'll just give her an injection."

He gave me some directions about dressings, said, "What a night!" and that he would look at her again in a couple of days.

"How long do you think she'll be lame?" I asked, thinking, she's due to go back in a fortnight.

He turned up his coat collar. His eyes were grey, his nose a little too large for the rest of his face.

"About ten days I should think. She isn't yours, is she?" he asked.

"No. I'm schooling her," I replied. It had stopped snowing. The wind was veering all ways, there was no saying what the weather would be tomorrow.

"How did it happen?" he asked, offering me a cigarette, lighting one for himself.

I told him about the shy, how I had fallen off, because I wasn't attending, what a fool I had been. It was a relief to tell someone, and he looked good-natured and friendly standing with his great coat pulled up round his ears. I felt better when I had finished.

"Jolly bad luck," he said. "It's the sort of thing which happens to everyone. If the professor turns nasty, let me know; I'll have a talk with him."

I said, "Thank you. I feel awful about it."

"Well, don't," he told me. "It isn't much. Are you going to the Hunt Ball?"

We talked about the ball for a few minutes before he got into his car, calling, "See you Friday," drove away, leaving tracks across the yard which lay like weals in the virgin snow.

I spoke to Fantasy, before I went indoors. The house seemed very quiet. I switched on the wireless, looked at the morning paper. I wanted to talk to Mummy about ringing up the professor, but I didn't want to put it off any longer.

In the end I went into the hall and dialled his number. Outside I could hear the trees creaking in the wind.

The professor answered himself. I said, "It's Jan Craigson speaking." I thought, this is awful. Supposing he's furious? "I'm afraid I've got some bad news," I continued. "Your mare came down this afternoon and grazed her hock. It isn't very bad, but I'm afraid it'll put her out of action for a few days."

"Oh I see," he said, not very agreeably. And I

thought, if he wants to know how it happened I shall have to admit I fell off.

"Have you had the vet? What does he say?" I told him what Mr. Strawley had done.

"What about insurance? Can I claim anything? She's insured, you know," he said.

I knew that. I never take horses otherwise, but it doesn't cover accidents.

"No, only if she dies or has to be put down," I told him. "Of course I shall keep her for nothing until she's fit again."

"I'm surprised that you should take her out in this weather," he said.

A few minutes later he rang off. He hadn't been exactly unpleasant, but the conversation had left a nasty taste in my mouth. The incident wasn't going to do my reputation any good. If only it could have happened to one of the other horses; their owners would have just said, "These things will happen," or, "What about you? Are you all right?" They wouldn't have made a fuss. I turned off the wireless and thought, it all depends on Benedictine. If he turns out all right and I win my pound, whatever the professor says won't matter much. But if he doesn't ... I didn't like to think of that.

I couldn't settle down. I roamed about the house picking things up and putting them down again. I felt in a muddle. On Saturday morning life had seemed normal. Guy didn't matter particularly; I didn't expect to go to the ball. I had hardly set eyes on Benedictine. Now my whole future seemed to hang in the balance.

Presently my parents returned. I told them about Fantasy as we ate supper.

"Don't worry, it'll turn out all right," Daddy said. "Things do in the end."

"Everyone in business has ups and downs," Mummy told me.

After supper I tried on my ball dress, which Mummy had cut out during the afternoon and was now held together with pins. It was early yet to tell how it would look when it was finished. But the materials hung superbly and the gold had a warm glow beneath the electric light. "I think it'll be very nice," Mummy said.

And I thought how near the ball was, and wondered whether I would ever be ready in time.

Much later I went to bed, and, looking out of the window, saw that it had stopped snowing and that there was a moon riding proudly aloof in a dark sky.

5

THE snow was still there next morning, though crisper now and somehow flatter. The wind had settled in the north-west.

I decided to leave the horses in and cut their oats and gave them hay with no clover in it.

Eleven o'clock found me at the hairdresser's with a magazine in my hand. Three hours later my hair was permed. I walked to the bus stop looking at myself in shop windows. I couldn't believe it was still me. I looked so different. I could only think, why didn't I have it done before? I stopped to buy an eyebrow pencil. Mummy had advised against mascara. "Leave it until you're a little older," she had said. I had a piece of my dress material with me. I bought a lipstick to match.

Angela was waiting for another bus in the

station. She waved and came across. "Gosh, what have you had done? You *do* look different."

"Do you like it? That's what matters," I replied.

"I should say so! I never knew you could look like that."

I was terrified now that I would bump into Guy or Chris. I wanted to surprise them both on Friday.

"You look like Diana Dors or Ingrid Bergman, or someone, I can't think who," Angela said.

"I'm too broad for that," I replied.

"I can't think who I mean. But it's someone," Angela said.

My bus came then. "Come to tea some time. I'll ring you up."

"That'll be lovely. Bye-bye," she said.

The sun was shining and in places the snow had begun to thaw. There was no one I knew on the bus.

I was very late for lunch. My hair met with Mummy's approval. During the rest of the afternoon I cleaned the tack, which was still dirty from Saturday.

There was only Thursday now between me and the Hunt Ball. I wondered whether I would ever be ready in time. I would have to get my clothes prepared for hunting; Velveteen well exercised, and on Friday Fantasy was to be gently walked round the yard. Domino couldn't go while there was still snow. The elements and fate seemed against me. Benedictine would be over-fresh and hysterical on Saturday if the snow didn't thaw soon.

But the next day was warm. The wind was in the southwest, the sky grey and blue. The snow turned to slush, and then to water which ran off the roof tops, dripped from the trees and gurgled into gutters and ditches along the roadside. As soon as the roads were clear, I rode Domino home. His owners, two girls of fifteen, threw their arms round his neck. Their mother gave me a glass of sherry and asked me whether it was true that I had the bay which had fallen on Sonia Stanmore.

I told them about Benedictine, explained that he wasn't vicious, but highly strung, that he was a horse in a thousand, and that Miss Peel was as honest as the day is long. I don't think they believed me. They thought I was a crony of Miss Peel's, and that I was on a fool's errand.

One of the girls said, "I'm glad I'm not you. Doesn't your mother object?"

"No, but she's a bit anxious," I admitted. "I think she's used to me taking risks though. I've been riding other people's horses and ponies since I was eight."

Presently they drove me home, and now the world seemed full of sunshine; the snow had all but disappeared, windows were open, people walked their dogs, pushed their prams and collected wood in the unexpected warmth of the day.

Bill Strawley was waiting for me in the stable yard.

As I waved goodbye to Domino's owners, he called, "Good morning to you. The mare is getting along nicely I think."

He was wearing corduroy trousers, a hacking jacket, a cloth cap.

"I'm so glad," I answered.

"How did the professor take it?" he asked.

We leaned against the stable wall and talked. It was that sort of morning. By the time he had gone, it was lunch time.

While the day was still warm I rode Benedictine. He was fresh and inclined to get behind his bit and I rode with a desperate firmness, driving him forward with my legs, and thinking of Saturday and how much there was at stake. Gradually he improved, his stride lengthened, his head dropped, his back relaxed, and now he was superb with the carriage and smoothness, the majesty and pace of a thoroughbred. I lunged Velveteen in the gathering dusk and resolved to ride him for two hours on the morrow.

After tea I tried on my dress which was all but finished. Except for length, it fitted perfectly. We had chosen a halter neckline and a flared skirt to minimise my hips. The halter halved the size of my shoulders; with my long hair and Mummy's earrings I was far from the Jan Craigson the Stanmores knew.

"You *do* look nice in it," Mummy said.

"What's this, a dress parade?" asked Daddy, stopping to peer round the door. "Oh whacko!"

There was a frost that night. The next morning was clear and sparkling. All trace of the snow had vanished. I wakened, thinking, it's today. The day has come. I couldn't stay in bed a moment longer.

I did the stables in record time. I could hardly eat any breakfast.

"Now do be sensible," Mummy said. "This may be your first ball, but it won't be your last. Relax."

"I'll try," I said.

I tried, but I couldn't. Tonight I was to wear my dress for the first time. I was going out to dinner. I was going to dance and Guy would be there. I schooled Benedictine for an hour, but I couldn't concentrate. I popped him over a few jumps which he cleared beautifully with heaps of scope. I rode Velveteen for two hours just as I had planned. I led Fantasy round the yard; I cleaned my tack and all the time one half of me was at the Hunt Ball. Time flew. All too soon it was tea time.

"Leave washing your gloves and things. I'll do them," Mummy offered.

Twilight had come slowly for a December evening, but now at five o'clock it was dark. I settled the horses for the night, checked my tack over for the morning. I had a long, gloriously hot bath, which left me drowsy, more fit for bed than a ball.

Since leaving the hairdresser's I had hardly touched my hair and it was sleek and somehow not quite mine any more.

At last I was ready and it was only just seven.

"Sit down and have a rest," said Mummy.

Daddy gave me a glass of sherry. "Remember not to mix your drinks," he told me with a smile. "Keep the grape and grain apart and don't forget, *Beer after wine makes you feel fine, Wine after beer makes you feel queer.*"

"I'm glad you're going with Chris," Mummy said.

I was trying not to think about tomorrow. I knew I should feel like the morning after the night before. It would be a bad time for improving my reputation. My hunting clothes were ready— Benedictine well exercised—there was nothing more I could do. But though the ball was uppermost in my mind, somewhere lurked the hunt, the bet and Benedictine. Could I, would I succeed?

Mummy fetched the biscuit tin, but I wasn't hungry. Daddy fetched me a cigarette.

"Don't forget to stand up for *God Save the Queen*," Mummy said. Then I heard a car.

"There's Chris," I cried, seizing Mummy's fur coat.

"Don't you want to ask him in?" Mummy asked.

I hadn't thought of that. I put down the coat, went to the front door and there was Chris on the doorstep, smiling in tails, white tie and white waistcoat.

"I was just about to knock," he said. "I'm afraid I'm early."

"So am I. Come in and have some sherry," I replied. My nerves had vanished. I felt completely self-possessed.

"You look marvellous," Chris said following me into the hall.

Both my parents had met Chris before, so introductions were unnecessary. Daddy poured out a glass of sherry and offered him a cigarette.

A few minutes later we were in the car, on our way to Summertown and a place Chris knew called The Falcon.

"You've changed your hair," he said.

"Do you like it?" I asked.

"You look different," he said.

Chris had borrowed his father's car. He drove very well in a decided competent way.

Summertown was nearly deserted. A few youths stood at street corners, two girls walked arm in arm, a couple lurked in a doorway. It was a brilliant night. The sky was dark with a million stars and over all hung the romance of a full moon.

To me nothing was quite real, not myself, nor Chris, nor the night; it all had a dream-like quality.

The Falcon was brilliantly lit. Chris parked the car with a flourish.

"I like driving, don't you?" he asked.

"I can't," I confessed.

"I'll teach you when I get my Baby Austin," he promised.

"When's that?" I asked.

"When I'm through my finals," he said.

Chris had booked a table. Somewhere someone was playing a violin. He took my coat and I saw that there were flowers on the tables and lamps made to look like candles.

"Let's cut out the sherry," Chris said. "What wine would you like?"

I didn't know. I hadn't expected Chris to be so sophisticated. Then I remembered that we had claret for Christmas.

"I like claret, but it depends on what we eat, doesn't it? I think you'd better choose."

Chris beamed at me across the table and I knew that I had said the right thing.

We took a long time over dinner. We discussed everything under the sun, without somehow coming any closer to one another.

"Gosh, we'll feel awful tomorrow," Chris said. "You realise that, don't you? The morning after the night before. I do think they might have made the meet later, don't you?"

"I don't suppose anyone will be punctual," I replied. I wanted to forget the morrow. It would come soon enough.

"*Have no thought for the morrow,*" I quoted.

We had reached the dessert.

"That comes from the Bible, doesn't it?" Chris asked.

"That's right," I said,

There were other people going on to the ball. Like us, they were in tails and long dresses. There was one large party with all the men in scarlet, and the women in jewellery and dresses which put mine to shame.

"They come from another pack. They're Londoners; can't you tell by their voices?" Chris said, following my glance.

After Chris's remark it didn't seem to matter that my dress couldn't rival theirs; we belonged to the hunt, they didn't, and that was what mattered. Presently people began to leave, women passed smelling of perfume, beautifully made up. The men were confident with a worldly air which Chris didn't possess.

The waiter came with the bill; another brought my coat. When we stepped outside the sky was just the same.

"There won't be much scent tomorrow," Chris remarked, tucking my dress into the car before he shut the door.

I remembered that tonight wasn't to be horsy and changed the subject. "What a heavenly night," I sighed, and thought, there's still so much of it left.

"When we return it will be morning," Chris said. And anything may have happened, I thought.

People were slamming car doors as we drove away from The Falcon and someone yelled, "All aboard? Let's get going then."

"They've sold every ticket," Chris told me.

I wanted that drive to last for ever. I seemed to hold time in my hand.

"There's going to be oysters, so if you mean to eat them, don't drink gin, or you'll be sick," Chris told me.

I had never eaten oysters. "How super," I said.

"You take one bite and swallow," Chris told me.

The road was very beautiful beneath the moon. It seemed to have added length and the tarmac wasn't ugly any more and even a row of hideous villas had a new dignity and an air of mystery in the moonlight.

The ball was being held in a country club and guest house, which was long and low and white, and had spacious lawns running down to the river, and an exciting reputation.

Tonight it was lit up, so that we could see its lights shining along the river while we were still half a mile away.

There were already twenty or thirty cars parked in the gravelled drive when we arrived.

"We are just right. I hate arriving early at dances, don't you?" Chris asked.

I had only been to Pony Club dances before and once to a village hop, and somehow, I had always managed to be a wallflower, so that I had returned home dismal and depressed with my scant self-confidence shaken to its roots. But tonight I meant things to be different.

"Yes," I said.

A man in uniform opened the car door. I stepped on to the gravel feeling like a million dollars. Inside the band was playing a waltz, and suddenly I was filled with an overwhelming impatience. I wanted to dance, to see Guy, to lose myself in the music and not think of anything beyond tonight.

I took Chris's arm. "Let's hurry," I said.

"All right, I'm coming. What's the rush?" he asked.

6

THE first person I saw was Sonia. She was giving her evening cloak to the attendant in the ladies' cloakroom. Her red hair was brushed back behind her ears; she wore long earrings and a black dress with red on the bodice.

"Oh hullo," she said. "How's the bay?"

I didn't want to talk horse, but I could hardly ignore her remark.

"Fine. How's your head?" I asked.

"Aches sometimes. I say, you're not really hunting him tomorrow, are you?"

"Yes, definitely, as long as there's hunting."

She turned away. "I see," was all she said.

Chris met me in the hall. There seemed to be flowers everywhere.

"Let's have a drink before we dance," he suggested.

Guy was in the bar buying Sonia a drink. I couldn't speak to him because there were too many heads between us. I don't think he saw me at first.

But presently he did and we smiled at each other over the heads and I thought he looked nice in evening dress.

Soon Chris and I were dancing together. The floor felt wonderful after the sitting room at home, and the music was the kind I like—light but not too light, the sort of music which makes you want to dance for ever.

After the dance we found our table. It was too near the band for conversation and Chris kept apologising.

I said, "It doesn't matter. I like watching the band anyway." But he kept remarking how stupid he had been.

The Maunders and the Stanmores had joined forces for the ball and as well as Guy, there were two young men in scarlet.

Chris and I danced together again and presently Bill Strawley came across to our table and said, "Hullo Jan. Meet Jean Waters."

He was holding Jean by the hand and I saw that she was dark with light brown eyes and a shy smile. I introduced Chris and we all sat down together and talked about the band, the other people and the buffet supper yet to come.

Chris and I danced again before we tackled the oysters. It was eleven o'clock by this time and I realised with despair how quickly the night was passing.

And then I saw Guy coming across the floor and noticed again how tall he was.

"Hullo. Isn't this fun? How's the bay?" he asked when he reached us.

"Wonderful. I like him more every day," I replied.

"Have a seat," Chris said, pulling out a chair.

We sat and talked until Guy turned to Chris and said, "Do you mind if we dance?"

In a moment we were dancing and Guy was saying, "You've altered your hair. You look different."

I said, "Do you like it?"

"Yes. It makes you look awfully glamorous," he said.

After that neither of us could think of anything to say for a time, until at last I said, "The band's good, isn't it?"

I could feel his breath on my cheek. My chin didn't quite reach his shoulder.

"Yes, quite. You've changed somehow. I suppose I've always seen you on a horse before. You dance beautifully too. Why haven't we danced together before?" he asked.

"I think we did once at a Pony Club dance when I was fourteen. I fell over your feet." I could remember it now, the surprise when he asked me, the discovery that I couldn't dance, the dismay afterwards.

"Did we? It must have been ages ago," he said.

I was pleased to see Chris dancing with a fair girl he evidently knew. It eased my conscience. I hadn't liked thinking of him sitting alone at our table.

Guy danced marvellously. And our pace and rhythm seemed to match, so that dancing together was like poetry.

I remember thinking, this is something I will always remember, whatever happens afterwards.

"You're with the Stanmores, aren't you?" I asked.

I wanted to find out how much he liked them.

"Yes, they asked us to join them some time ago," he said.

And now the waltz had finished. We stood poised for a moment and then turned to clap like everyone else.

Guy met my eyes and smiled. "Come and be introduced to the people you don't know," he said, taking my hand.

I felt very adult as I walked across the floor with Guy. I felt very self-possessed. Approaching the Stanmores hand in hand with Guy freed me completely of any sense of inferiority. I didn't mind if they thought me horsy now.

The Stanmores looked up as we approached.

"It is Jan. I said it was," Audrey exclaimed.

Susan and one of the young men in scarlet were dancing. Guy introduced me to the other and to his own father and mother. I glanced at my table and saw with relief that Chris was still dancing.

"We didn't recognise you, in evening dress," Audrey said. "We hear you *are* hunting Benedictine on Saturday."

"Yes. Is that all right?" I asked, because after all he was their horse.

"Of course, that's the bargain," Audrey said. "I'm expecting to win a pound."

Guy poured me a glass of champagne.

"I only hope you don't hurt yourself," said Mrs. Stanmore.

Guy's father was dark with grey eyes. He made conversation in presumably the same voice as he used in the House of Commons, which was rather loud and as though he was addressing an inattentive audience. Guy's mother was charming with beautifully done grey hair, brown eyes and an air of being perpetually amused.

She said, "I've heard so much about you, Jan. Do sit down."

I thought, Guy must have told her and felt a rush of happiness and thought, perhaps he does like me and saw us going out together, Guy telephoning, saying, "Are you free tonight, Jan?"

I sat and talked and when the conversation turned to horses I didn't mind, nor try to change it.

Presently Guy and I danced together again. And he said, "You know I'm going overseas soon. Isn't it hell when we've just met?"

I felt a knot in my throat which seemed to grow larger every moment. I asked, "How soon?" and he said, "Almost any day now," and then smiled. "Well, not tomorrow anyway. I shall see who wins the bet."

I thought of tomorrow, of the dawn which would come as I reached home, of bed and getting up again and the day which was to mean so much to me.

While I danced with Guy it didn't seem to matter, but in the morning it would, and I should need all my small amount of skill to keep Benedictine going properly.

"I don't care much about the pound," I said. "My reputation matters a bit, but most of all I care about Benedictine."

"You really think he's all right?" Guy asked.

"Yes. I think he has tremendous possibilities."

"I only hope you're right," said Guy, and he sounded sad, as though he thought I had made a grave error.

I felt terribly alone then. No one believed in Benedictine but myself and Miss Peel. And then I remembered that Guy would soon be overseas and I said, "I suppose the Stanmores will let you know what happens to him eventually."

"I expect so," he replied.

I could see Chris sitting alone at our table. I looked at him and Guy said, "Do you think you ought to go back?"

"I suppose so," I said.

We went back together.

"I'll see you tomorrow then," Guy told me. He smiled at Chris.

"Yes, on Benedictine I hope," I replied, and then wondered whether I sounded boastful. I hoped not.

"Hullo. You looked fine dancing together," Chris said without malice.

"I'm sorry to have left you for so long," I told him, my eyes following Guy for an instant across the room to the Stanmores' tables.

"That's all right. I found a great friend of mine, Sheila Simmons. Do you know her?"

I said I didn't. Somehow the evening seemed a little flat now that I had danced with Guy.

Presently the buffet was open and Chris and I collected plates of delicious lobster salad, and meringues with cream.

After that we danced again. And then sat in silence, because we knew each other well enough for that.

Then the band began to liven up. They played the gallop and there were cries of "Do you ken John Peel" and lots of holloas and I saw Guy whirling Audrey round and round with his hair askew. And Chris seized a hunting horn from someone's table and blew it. The owner returned and there was an undignified scuffle and a girl said, "Aren't they awful? I believe they're drunk."

I think she thought they were really fighting.

After a time Chris gave up the horn and we continued dancing and hours later there was the last dance and I looked for Guy without seeing him. Everybody was a little mad by this time. One girl had lost a shoe and someone upset a table. And then suddenly there was "Auld Lang Syne" and I stood thinking, it's over, but at least I danced with Guy.

Chris had Sheila Simmons on the other side of him and he was smiling at her. The lights were dim. I still couldn't see Guy. *God Save the Queen* followed, and then there were sausages and soup. The band were packing up their instruments; to all intents and purposes the ball was over.

Chris chanted:

> "After the ball was over
> She took out her one glass eye,
> Put her false teeth in the basin,
> Corked up her bottles of dye.

Stood her false leg in the corner,
Hung her false wig on the wall,
And all that was left went to bye-byes
After the ball."

He looked very happy. "Wasn't it funny bumping into Sheila again? I haven't seen her for ages," he said.

"Yes, she looks nice," I said.

"She's a sweet girl," agreed Chris.

The soup was very hot. It was four o'clock in the morning. I could hear the chink of plates and people laughing as they washed up. It's over, I thought, all over.

" 'Night, Jan, 'night Chris," called Bill Strawley. "Have a good day tomorrow."

He looked enormous in a dark coat, white scarf, pigskin gloves.

"Thanks, we will," said Chris.

"Don't break your neck, Jan," he called back.

And then I saw Guy smiling at me. He waved his hand in salute. "See you tomorrow, Jan. Look after yourself." I smiled back at him and called, "I will. Goodbye."

I think I was very happy then. I remember collecting Mummy's coat in a kind of dream and wishing that it was Guy who was to drive me home, though I was fond enough of Chris.

Outside the brilliant night was giving place to a grey dawn. It was very cold. Chris wrapped a rug round my knees as soon as I was in the car. And I remember feeling suddenly sleepy. Everyone was leaving and it was some time before we were clear of the drive. Somewhere a cock was crowing.

"It was fun, wasn't it?" Chris asked.

"Tremendous. My first Hunt Ball. Thank you so much for taking me," I replied.

"It was a pleasure," Chris said.

I couldn't put off thinking about the morning any longer; it had come. Every moment the sky was growing a little lighter; there was a faint breeze; it looked as though scenting conditions would be perfect.

I shan't plait, I thought, there won't be time. Already I was seeing the meet, Benedictine and myself standing outside the Three Horse Shoes. I think I prayed then that he would behave, as much for my own sake as for his.

"Gosh, it's colder. I wish this car had a heater," complained Chris.

"I'm lovely and warm," I said, and it was true, only somewhere far down inside I was cold and empty and a little frightened.

I thought, I shall take some aspirins when I get home. I must sleep.

"Should be plenty of scent," murmured Chris.

"Heaps," I agreed, seeing hounds in full cry, hearing the horn, thinking I'll keep him going, I won't give him a chance to go up even if he thinks of it. There was a cat running stealthily along Summertown High Street.

Otherwise nothing moved. We heard an alarm clock as we drove through the suburbs.

"We must do it again," Chris said. "We seem to be able to dance together."

"I'd love to," I said. But I felt he didn't mean it; next he would ask Sheila Simmons. Chris could never make the sun shine for me, nor me for him. We were simply good companions.

"Here we are," he said, stopping the car, jumping out, opening the door for me.

"Thank you so very much," I said.

He came to the front door with me. "Would you like to come in for a drink or anything—a cup of tea?" I asked. I didn't know what one did after a ball. I had no experience to help me. Should I offer bacon and eggs?

He touched my arm. "No thank you all the same. I think I ought to be getting along. Can you get in all right?"

For a moment I couldn't find my key, while Chris waited anxiously, saying, "What about a pocket? Do you think it's in the car?" I found it mixed up with my handkerchief in my evening bag.

We both sighed with relief. "Sorry to be such a drip," I said.

We thanked each other again, before I let myself into the house and he drove away into the dawn. Suddenly I was very tired, too tired even for bed. I stood and looked at myself in the mirror and wondered when I should wear my dress again. I remembered everything Guy had said, the intonation of his voice, the emphasis he had put on each word.

I thought of the things I might have said and done, before I heard footsteps padding along the passage. A second later Mummy's head was round the door. She must have been listening for the car.

"Did you have a good time, darling?" she asked.

She came in and sitting on my bed we discussed the ball. It was lovely to have someone to talk things over with; and, though I did not tell her about my feelings for Guy, I think she guessed a lot.

Some time later I fell into bed and was instantly asleep, while beside me the alarm clock ticked on relentlessly, bringing the meet and all that was to follow nearer each passing second.

7

I REMEMBER waking with the waltz I danced with Guy ringing in my ears, thinking what happened? Remembering.

Then the alarm went off.

It was really morning now. Grey clouds hung low in the sky. The wind veered between north and south-west. The postman was delivering mail. The milk had come.

It's today, I thought, dressing, feeling limp, wondering what would happen. Mummy handed me a mug of coffee as I went through the kitchen. I had no time to waste. It was eight o'clock and I needed to be on the road by ten.

I said, "Thank you," and realised that my head was muzzy, and thought, I must hurry. I mustn't stop. There's no time for talk.

The horses whinnied to me. I rushed round the stables, dropping things, losing things, upsetting the wheelbarrow just as it was full. I felt my temper fraying and knew that I must keep calm if I was to win my pound and save Benedictine. And now the weather seemed unbearably warm. Why wasn't there a wind, a tang in the air, something which would stimulate me?

I was still half asleep as I gobbled breakfast.

"Don't try to talk. Tell us everything tonight," Mummy said. I gave her a grateful smile.

"And go carefully," Daddy said. "Remember a pound is of no great importance."

"I'll remember," I promised. And now breakfast was finished I groomed Benedictine. He looked taller than ever. I could hardly reach his withers. I fetched his tack, put it on, filled up the other horses' water buckets, checked their hay, went indoors and dressed. There was still a nasty nagging feeling in the pit of my stomach. It seemed as though it would be with me always. Would life ever be peaceful again? I wondered.

So far I had hardly thought of Guy, but as I dressed, what he had said and our dance together came back to me. Was he getting ready too? I wondered. Did he get Prudence ready himself, or was there a groom? How little I knew about him. I wished for hunting clothes again as I pulled a jersey over my head. I remembered to put a pound in my pocket, because the impossible might happen. I couldn't imagine myself giving it to Sonia. It would be horribly embarrassing. If it happened would everyone be there watching?

I clattered downstairs, apologised for not helping with the washing up. I mounted, waved goodbye, rode out into December day, and feeling Benedictine beneath me restored my confidence; hacking along country roads, calling, "Good morning," to everyone on foot or bicycle, failure seemed impossible.

Benedictine walked with a long swinging stride, the reins were supple beneath my fingers, above me the sky was growing lighter each moment, in front the fields were bleak and bare, but friendly too, and in a tree a bird sang.

I was in plenty of time. There were sandwiches in my pocket, a spare pair of gloves beneath the girth. Never had disaster seemed so distant. After a time I was singing the tunes of the night before. Benedictine cocked his long ears backwards and forwards, his stride grew longer still, his eyes were shining, he felt completely happy.

So we came to the meet at the Three Horse Shoes. We weren't the first to arrive; there were already five or six horsemen, a crowd on foot, children, dogs, prams. A broad-shouldered farmer was drinking beer, a small girl was giving an even smaller village child a ride on her pony. Of Guy and Chris there was as yet no sign. I rode Benedictine up and down outside the pub.

A farmer called, "That's the Stanmores' bay, isn't it?"

"That's right," I answered.

"Said it was," he said.

Hounds came next, bright and smiling, the huntsman and whip laughing together, the two terriers running with the pack. Tom called, "Morning, Missy, it's true then you've got the bay."

"That's right," I said.

"You've got a nerve," he said.

Benedictine was trembling with excitement now. I patted his neck, rode him up and down. The next few minutes would be the worst. Once we were hunting I was convinced he wouldn't think of rearing. But now, while we had to stand about, he might go up through sheer impatience.

They were very long, those minutes at the Meet. I wished that I had started later or dawdled more on the way. My nerves were terribly on edge and the same empty feeling was nagging at my stomach.

Two more horsemen turned up and then the Stanmores in full force. Benedictine looked at their horses and whinnied and I thought he mustn't go up now and trotted away down the road.

When I returned Chris and Captain Williams

had arrived. I waved to them all and then hounds moved off.

"You look sleepy, Jan," the Master said.

"I am," I replied, rubbing my eyes.

Presently Guy came tearing down the road after us. He hadn't bothered to put on hunting clothes, but wore jodhs, a hacking jacket, and a polo-necked jersey.

"I suppose you've only just crawled out of bed," Sonia said.

"That's right," Guy replied, smiling at me, saying, "He looks all right at the moment, Jan."

"Touch wood," I replied.

"You wait," Sonia said.

We came to the first covert, a beech wood lying in a valley. And now the sun was shining, and I took off my gloves.

"What a marvellous day," Chris said.

Tom put hounds in. The whip disappeared towards a far corner. "Keep your fingers crossed, Jan," Sonia said.

But Benedictine was standing like a rock; his head was up, his ears pricked. He was relaxed and happy and I felt a wave of immense relief. The best part of the day would be the end when I could ride home knowing that I was right and there was nothing more to worry about; but now I felt absurdly happy. I had danced with Guy. Benedictine was behaving himself. Listening to Tom encouraging hounds, watching the sun play on the horses' bits, I felt that the world was a marvellous place. It was a long time before a hound spoke and all that time Benedictine stood like a sentry on watch. It was almost as though he knew how much was at stake.

When the first hound spoke, Tom blew an encouraging note on the horn. Then we heard a holloa and Captain Williams cried, "He's broken on the far side." And Tom blew the gone away and there was a terrific crash of music, and then we were all galloping round the outside of the wood with mud flying, hoofs pounding and the wind behind us.

"What luck. In the first covert too," Chris cried. Benedictine was going like a dream. He had a better gallop than any other horse I had ever ridden, long, low, full of immense power, the sort of gallop that carries you over a plough without faltering, which will last all day and still be there at the end.

We could all see hounds now streaming away into the open beyond the wood. They were bunched together, a mass of black, tan and white, a blob of colour in the December landscape. Tom was leaning forward, doubling the horn, a small scarlet figure on a big brown horse. He seemed to belong to the landscape too, along with the music, the pack and the thundering hoofs. In the distance a herd of cows stood huddled in a corner. A man stood hollering by a gate. The sun had gone; above the sky had turned a darker grey.

We came to a gate in a wire fence, which Chris opened; then we were galloping on across stubble. In front was a line of rails, not very high, but formidable, because they were thick and firm and stout enough to turn a horse over if he hit them.

We took them slowly. No one fell. Benedictine lengthened his stride, took off feet away and still cleared them with heaps to spare. We turned right and Chris said, "He's going beautifully, Jan. Keep it up."

"I'll try," I answered, leaning forward to pat Benedictine, thinking if only nothing happens, already seeing my triumphant return.

Soon we were on grass again, galloping towards a lane fenced on each side by hedges. And now Guy was beside me and we were riding shoulder to shoulder, knee to knee. "Did you get back all right?" he asked, shouting against the sound of hoofs.

"Yes, thanks. Getting up this morning was the worst part of everything," I replied.

"I know. I haven't even groomed Prudence. Does she look awful?" he asked.

I was in heaven now. "No, I don't think so. She's too hot to tell anyway. Besides, no one's likely to notice after last night," I said.

"That's comforting," said Guy.

We had reached the lane. "Looks as though we'll have to jump in and out," he said.

"We'd better take it slowly," I answered.

Further down Captain Williams was already jumping. "Do be careful," cried Guy as I collected Benedictine.

I took the hedge slowly, and Benedictine, as clever as a cat, jumped neatly into the lane and out again.

A moment later we were galloping on together again and Guy was saying, "I believe you're right about that horse. He goes superbly. He looks quite different when you're on top."

We jumped another hedge, swung left through a farmyard, where the farmer and his wife stood waving by their house. Last night seemed far away. Nothing mattered now except myself and Guy galloping together with the same music in both our ears, the same wind on our backs, and the same landscape stretched before us. Galloping then I felt that everything was with me, the wind, fate, luck, opportunity. I was certain now that soon I should have an extra pound, Benedictine would be saved, my reputation would soar, Miss Peel's be restored. I was incredibly, madly happy.

Hounds checked at last in a little covert by the river.

Here the day seemed bleaker and the sky darker.

"Jolly good, Jan," Chris called.

The Stanmores seemed to be avoiding me. I felt that my victory was nearly complete. I even felt a little sorry for them.

When Captain Williams said, "Will you just slip round the far side of the covert?" I felt no qualm of anxiety. I had long ago decided that nothing could go wrong today.

"Shall I go with her?" Guy asked.

"No, one's enough," Captain Williams replied.

Benedictine left the other horses without hesitation. The ground was squelchy, the wind in my face. I reached the far side and in the distance I could see the gasworks and suburbs of Summertown. There wasn't much noise from the covert; hounds seemed to have lost their fox completely. Benedictine stood very still, as though he had been hunting all his life. My watch told me that it was one o'clock.

I remember thinking, this is one of the best hunts I've ever known, and seeing Guy again in tails pouring me champagne. Then a hound spoke and my attention became riveted to the covert. Presently another hound spoke and then another; my blood started to run faster and Benedictine began to tremble. Tom blew a short toot on his horn. A shrill voice screamed, "Tally ho." They're breaking into the open, I decided. I turned Benedictine. At the same moment Tom blew the gone away.

I didn't go the way I had come, because hounds were obviously breaking on the other side. I galloped straight on along the covert, swung left and saw a stream in front of us. I hesitated for a moment. I didn't know whether Benedictine had ever jumped water; then I remembered that he had never stopped at anything yet. I pushed him into a gallop and heard hoofs thundering away into the distance. It was obvious that Benedictine and I would have to hurry if we were to catch up with the field again.

As I approached the stream I saw that it was larger than I had supposed, but still I didn't hesitate. I pushed Benedictine on, leaned forward, waited for him to take off. I heard the horn again and then Benedictine seemed to stumble, I grabbed his mane and had time to think, what's happening? before he crumpled under me. I saw dark dirty water, smelt dead reed and slimy mud before I hit the further bank with my shoulder. I saw him struggling before he scrambled to his feet and leapt from the stream to the bank. His hoofs missed me by less than an inch. It was the most terrifying moment of my life.

I was filled with a ghastly sense of catastrophe as I scrambled to my feet. My shoulder hurt abominably. The day which had begun with so much promise now seemed black indeed.

Benedictine was fast disappearing in pursuit of

hounds. His speed which I had admired with so much enthusiasm now became a disadvantage. I prayed that he wouldn't reach the field before myself without much conviction. My coat was plastered with mud; my head ached; my shoulder had lost all feeling.

I remembered then that *Pride comes before a fall*. I stumbled wearily across the endless water meadow and in front were Benedictine's hoof prints clear and deep in the soft ground. I thought, you had this coming to you, Jan Craigson, but it didn't make anything any better. I wondered what the Stanmores would say when they saw Benedictine approaching riderless. Would they believe me when I said he hadn't reared?

I was feeling sick now and I took out my handkerchief and thought, don't be a fool, don't cry. I thought, at least the professor isn't out. Maybe a farm hand will catch Benedictine. Then I thought, supposing he gets on the road and hurts himself like Fantasy? I decided then that I wasn't fit to take other people's horses to school.

I heard the horn again, faint and far away. I came to an open gate and entered another field as vast as the first. Here there were hundreds of hoofprints and a stray hound who hurried past, a guilty expression on his face.

I remembered how triumphant I had felt less

than fifteen minutes ago, though now it seemed much longer.

I remembered how Guy and Chris had congratulated me, how it had seemed like a perfect day. I started to run and remembered how I had run after Fantasy in the snow and I thought, you're going to pieces, Jan. I think I began to cry then; I was suddenly so tired. The ball and the early morning, the excitement and suspense, seemed to have sapped all my energy so that now when I really needed it, I had none left.

8

I CAME at last to the river, to pretty cottages with creepers on their walls, to more green fields, a road and a wooden bridge. I stood and looked and wondered. There was no sign of the hunt any more, nothing to guide me to Benedictine. The sky was darker; there was a mist in the air. My watch told me that it was two o'clock.

I remember standing suddenly too miserable to care any more, while the tunes of the night before played crazily in my head and somewhere there was room for despair.

Then a man leaned out of a pub further along the road. "Are you looking for the hunt?" he called.

"Yes, I am," I answered, realising what a miserable figure I must cut with dirty, tear-stained face, mud-spattered coat, and a shoulder which didn't seem to work any more.

"They went over the bridge about fifteen minutes ago," he said.

I thought, they'll be in the next county by now. I called, "Thank you," walked on over the bridge, wondering how I would ever be able to face anyone again.

There were fat Jersey cows grazing by the river. They raised their heads and looked at me with soft placid eyes.

For a moment I envied them their obvious content, then I thought I heard the horn and started to run again.

There were plenty of hoofprints to guide me now. And then at last I saw horses in the distance. I broke into a walk and wondered what I would say. Would the Stanmores believe me? How could I ask for my pound now?

Gradually the horses and riders grew larger and I saw that they were all standing together in the middle of a field. I realised then that they had killed. I had missed everything. I stopped to wipe my face; I didn't want anyone to know that I had cried; after all I was seventeen. I pushed my hair further under my hat, wiped my dirty hands on damp grass. I thought, I can only tell the truth and if I look a fool, what does it matter? But it did matter. My good name and business were involved. Soon unless things improved, no one would send me their horses to school. My loose boxes would be empty, no hoofs would fire sparks on the Staffordshire bricks, I should be out of work. I should have to begin again in a new profession.

I saw Chris leave the others. I saw him wave and knew that he had seen me. He came galloping towards me, dramatic against the dark sky.

"Hallo. What happened?" he called.

"We fell into a stream," I shouted.

He drew rein and I saw Sonia following with Benedictine. "Bad luck," she called, rather as though I had lost a tennis match.

"I'm sorry," said Chris with sympathy in his grey eyes.

"He didn't rear. We fell into a stream," I said.

"I think you were jolly plucky to take him on at all," exclaimed Sonia.

"He didn't rear," I repeated.

"Oh good, you're still in the running for the pound then," said Chris.

"I wouldn't ride him again if I were you," Sonia told me.

I could feel my temper rising. She didn't believe me, because she didn't want to believe me.

"Why shouldn't I ride him?" I asked. I was frightened of myself. I didn't want to say much.

Benedictine, after all, still belonged to the Stanmores.

I couldn't see Guy. Perhaps he had gone home. Perhaps this was his last hunt, perhaps I wouldn't see him again for years.

"He's lost a stirrup and leather. You'd better have one of mine," Chris said.

I could see Audrey and Susan approaching. There were pins and needles in my shoulder and my whole left arm was beginning to ache and there was a sinking feeling inside me, because Guy had gone without saying goodbye.

I took Benedictine from Sonia with my left hand, and Chris said, "What's the matter? Have you hurt your right arm?"

"It's a bit stiff, that's all. I must have fallen on it," I replied.

"I think he's a perfectly beastly horse," cried Susan, drawing rein alongside the rest of us. "First it's Sonia and now he's hurt Jan."

"He's just no good," said Audrey.

"It was my fault. I put him at a stream and he's obviously never jumped water before," I said, but I felt as though I was fighting a losing battle.

"I don't care what happened. I still think he's a beastly horse," said Audrey.

Chris was taking off one of his stirrups and leathers.

I said, "Don't bother, Chris. I can manage all right. Honestly I can."

"Don't be silly," he replied and I could see that he meant to be chivalrous and nothing I could say would stop him. I patted Benedictine. "We'd better hurry. They'll be moving off soon," Audrey said.

"Did they kill?" I asked.

"Yes, didn't you hear? Tom blew the rattle extra loud so that you would know where we were," Susan told me.

I mounted trying not to use my right arm. I rode on with Chris and the Stanmores. I thought, I can't ask for my pound now.

Captain Williams called, "Are you all right, Jan?" They had been waiting for us; now hounds moved off along the river towards an osier bed. Benedictine was very quiet.

"Yes, thank you. We fell in a stream," I told Captain Williams. Did he believe me? I wondered. It was impossible to tell. His face was quite impassive.

"I'm sorry," was all he said.

I thought, I shan't stay out much longer. More than anything, I longed for a cup of tea, a hot bath and a sympathetic ear. Chris stayed near me. We came to the osier bed. Tom put hounds in. Benedictine stood like a rock.

"He's a handsome horse, Jan," Captain Williams said. There was no sign of Guy.

"Well, you haven't lost your pound anyway," Chris said, and I knew I must be looking miserable and that he was trying to cheer me up.

"No, but I shan't win it whatever happens, not now," I replied.

"But you should," Chris said. "I shall speak to the Stanmores."

I said, "Please don't," but already Chris was riding to where the three girls stood talking. I remembered my sandwiches, held the reins in my teeth and fished them out of my pocket with my left hand.

I heard Chris say, "But he didn't rear." And I rode away because I was sick of the subject; I wanted to forget the stream and the whole tiresome incident.

I stood under a tree and ate my sandwiches alone. Benedictine stood watching the osier bed and the other horses with wisdom in his eyes. I patted his bay neck and wondered why I had bothered to become involved with a horse which didn't concern me, but knew that if the same opportunity arose again I should do exactly the same.

There wasn't a fox in the osier bed. Chris came across to where I stood.

"They're being cagey," he said.

"That's putting it mildly," I replied.

I think I hated the Stanmores then. They had never bothered to ride properly. They had no real sympathy for their horses, only sentiment. They were terrified of being horsy. And yet they could condemn a horse like Benedictine on one rear.

"Let's be honest, they don't believe me, do they?" I asked.

"No, I don't think they do," said Chris.

It is awful not to be believed. It leaves you so helpless. There seems nothing you can do. I remember I felt like riding up to the Stanmores and screaming, "I tell you he didn't rear, he didn't, he didn't, didn't, didn't." Then my anger cooled, and I was left with nothing but a miserable flat feeling.

Chris looked at my face and said, "I'll see if I can fix a compromise."

I said, "You're marvellous, Chris. You ought to be a diplomat."

Tom was blowing hounds out of the osiers. No one seemed interested in the hunt any more. They had galloped enough and there wasn't much chance of finding a fox so late in the day. The mist had cleared. It was a fine afternoon for December. I glanced at my watch and saw that it was after three. Soon we would be turning for home.

Chris and the Stanmores appeared to be arguing. Tom and the Master were deciding where to draw next. Guy must be home by now, I thought, and he'll never know what happened today except from the Stanmores' point of view. I think that it was then that

I decided to write to him; because I wanted him to know the true story.

Chris came back. "I've said you'll hunt him again next Saturday. Is that all right?" he asked.

"Yes," I replied, wondering what had happened to my shoulder, hoping that it would have recovered by then.

Chris rode back to the Stanmores. Tom and the whip counted hounds before moving off. I rode on with the field. I didn't want to speak to anyone; my heart felt as heavy as lead.

Hounds didn't find again. Forty minutes later the Master decided to call it a day. I didn't speak to the Stanmores. I didn't feel that I ever wanted to speak to them again. They probably felt the same about me.

As I turned for home, Captain Williams called, "Good luck, Jan," as though he knew what had happened and was on my side.

Chris said, "I'll ride some of the way with you."

We rode back along the river and evening came, warm and friendly.

"I'm sorry, Jan," Chris said.

"It doesn't matter," I told him. "I'll simply have to try again next Saturday."

"It's such a pity, because he went so marvellously today," he said.

We weren't sure of the way home, but we asked a

farm hand and later a fat woman with a shopping basket.

Darkness came as we reached familiar roads. Our horses walked happily side by side. We rode in silence mostly, only once discussing the Hunt Ball. I think we both were so sick of the Stanmores, that we only wanted to forget them.

Presently we parted and Chris said, "Be careful, won't you?"

And I said, "Thank you for everything," and gave him back his stirrup and leather.

"See you on Saturday if not before," he called over his shoulder, riding away, leaving Benedictine and myself alone on the dark familiar road.

Twenty minutes later I was home. I put Benedictine away. My arm was even stiffer. My shoulder was quite numb. I found I couldn't lift a bucket, except with my left hand. Mummy came out into the yard. "What sort of day did you have?" she asked.

I didn't want to upset her over my arm. "Middling," I replied. I think I sounded offhand and rather squashing. I didn't mean to. Actually I felt as though I wanted to cry on her shoulder; I wanted to crawl into bed and have her tuck me up as though I was a child again.

"Well, tea's ready when you are," Mummy told me.

It was ages before I had settled all the horses. I

staggered into the kitchen wishing that I had never been to the Hunt Ball, nor hunting, wishing more than anything that I had a secure job bringing in a steady wage packet each week.

I sat down at the kitchen table with my head in my hands. "Here, have a cup of tea," Mummy said, fetching the tea pot, filling a cup.

I sipped the tea. "It was an awful day actually," I said. I began to tell her of what had happened. I was trying all the time not to cry again. I suppose it was the effect of the ball and then the hunt on top of it. I don't often want to cry.

Mummy listened with her eyes on my face. When I had finished, she said, "I think we ought to take you in and get your arm X-rayed."

Then she said, "Poor Jan," and put her arm round me, and said, "I wouldn't bother about the Stanmores; they aren't worth it."

I think I cried a bit then. I remember blowing my nose anyway, and telling myself that I was seventeen and too old for tears.

"Why didn't you tell me before, you silly," Mummy said. "I could have helped you with the horses."

"I didn't want to upset you," I said.

There were lots of little rock cakes just out of the oven, and hunks of bread and butter and honey and jam. I ate a good tea and began to feel better.

"It's awful not to be believed. I'm not surprised you were upset," Mummy said.

Presently Daddy came in, and Mummy told him the story and then rang up for a car because we haven't got one.

"Do I really need to go to the hospital then?" I asked.

"Yes, without a doubt," Daddy said.

Mummy tried to brush some of the mud off my coat. Then the car came.

It was a dismal drive. Before we had travelled a hundred yards, I was asleep. There were three people waiting in the Casualty Department at the hospital; a man who had put his knee out playing football and a couple who had come off a motor bike.

My turn came last. There were magazines to read, bustling nurses to watch, doctors in white coats. I think I fell asleep again. I know it didn't seem long before I was talking to a young curly-headed doctor. I thought he was a foreigner, but afterwards Mummy said his accent was Lancashire. He had blue eyes. He felt my shoulder. "You've been hunting then?" he asked. His hands were firm and skilful.

"Yes, that's right," I said.

"Did you have a nice day? I used to ride when I was a boy."

"Middling. Actually it was quite a good day. I spoilt it for myself by falling off," I told him.

"Tough luck. I'm afraid you may have broken something," he said. "We'd better get you X-rayed."

The other casualties had gone home. I followed the doctor into a large light room full of apparatus. A woman in a white coat took three X-rays. Outside it was raining. I thought suddenly of Guy. Was he packing? I thought of the opportunities that I had missed and remembered that *Too late* and *If only* are the saddest words in the English language.

"I'm afraid you'll have to wait till they're developed," the doctor said.

We went back to the Casualty Department and looked at the magazines again.

"Doesn't it all take ages?" Mummy said.

"Yes, hours," I agreed, thinking of the morning, of the ride to the meet and how hopeful I had been.

"One never knows what's going to happen, does one?" I asked.

"That's what makes life such fun," Mummy said.

The magazines were very out of date, the bench we sat on incredibly hard.

At last a nurse said, "This way, Miss Craigson." She was young, with a tiny waist and curls which crept from under her cap. She was very pretty.

"Do sit down," said the doctor indicating two chairs. We both sat down. You could hear the rain beating against the window. There was a bed with a bucket underneath. Everything smelt of antiseptic.

"I'm afraid you've broken your collar bone, Miss Craigson," he said.

I thought, oh damn! How can I ride Benedictine with a broken collar bone? But I must, I've got to hunt next Saturday. I said, "Oh, I see."

"Oh dear," exclaimed Mummy.

"It's an exceedingly mild break," he said, "I'll strap it up for you. But you mustn't use your right arm for a bit."

"Poor Jan. No wonder it felt funny," Mummy said.

I didn't feel like crying now. I felt hopelessly angry. I took off my coat and jersey again, and wondered why I had to break my collar bone at such an important time.

"Tell me if I'm hurting," the doctor said.

I bit my lip and thought about Guy. Presently he said, "There you are then. Come back at once if it hurts a lot."

The nurse gave me an appointment. Mummy shook hands with the doctor. We thanked them both.

Outside it was raining quite hard.

"It's a good thing we came in," Mummy said.

It was ages before we found a taxi. We were both really wet by then and my teeth were chattering.

"You're going to have supper in bed," Mummy said.

"I shall have to finish the horses first," I replied.

"No you won't. Duncan and I will see to them," Mummy told me.

Duncan is Daddy's Christian name.

The taxi driver grumbled about the weather, about the cost of living, about almost everything.

Daddy met us on the front porch. "Well, what's the verdict?" he asked.

Mummy told him. I didn't want to talk any more. I just wanted to sleep. I felt as though I hadn't been to bed for hours though it was only eight o'clock.

Mummy brought me supper in bed, and Daddy brought a hot drink with whisky in it. Outside the rain beat hard against my bedroom window. Mercifully I was too tired to think, if I had I hate to think of the conclusions I might have reached. As soon as I had finished supper I fell asleep, with the tray on my knees; why it didn't fall on the floor is one of the things I've never understood.

I didn't hear Mummy come in and switch off the light. I was dead to the world, too tired even for dreams.

9

I WAKENED next morning and it was still raining. My shoulder was stiff, and yesterday came back to me with hideous clarity ... . I thought, I'd better get up. I felt limp and I had an awful sense of having missed something. For a moment I couldn't think why. Then I remembered that Guy had gone without saying goodbye.

I got out of bed then and looked at myself in the mirror. My face was pale and there was some mud on my forehead. I thought, everything's gone wrong, Benedictine, Guy, myself. I sat on the bed again and tried to think; that I must continue riding was obvious, and there was no reason why I shouldn't manage it in one hand. Grooming and feeding the horses was more of a problem, but somehow I would manage. My watch told me it was eight o'clock. There was no sound from the kitchen, nor from the bathroom where Daddy would generally be having his bath at this time. I wondered what had happened. I drew back my curtains and then I knew—in the stable yard Mummy and Daddy were mucking out the boxes. Mummy was wearing a pair of my dungarees turned up at the bottoms and secured by a belt, Daddy had on his oldest trousers and a fisherman's jersey. They were in a great hurry. Obviously they wanted to have everything done before I appeared. I sat on my bed for a moment after that and thought how wonderful my parents were and tried to imagine Mr. and Mrs. Stanmore cleaning out boxes for their daughters. I thought, if I have children I shall try to be as good as they are, and then I dressed and went downstairs and out into the yard.

"Hullo," cried Mummy, "you're just in time. We've just finished."

I didn't know what to say. Daddy was putting the tools away; he looked like a tall fair-skinned Swedish fisherman.

I said, "Thank you so much, you shouldn't have bothered." It sounded hopelessly inadequate and it didn't say what I felt.

"Gosh, that black is a bad-tempered brute!" exclaimed Daddy wiping his hands on the seat of his trousers. "He nearly bit me twice."

I had to laugh then. I thought of Daddy dodging Velveteen.

"You heartless girl," Daddy said.

"Thank you so much," I said again.

"Don't mench," Daddy replied. "I enjoyed it—made me feel years younger."

We went indoors. My sense of failure had vanished; suddenly it was good to be alive. At least I've got a second chance with Benedictine, I thought, and if I don't see Guy again it won't be the end of the world.

Daddy disappeared to change. Mummy and I got breakfast. The kitchen was wonderfully warm. Mummy looked very young in my dungarees, her hair was wet, and rain glistened on her cheeks.

"How do you feel?" she asked.

"Fine, thank you," I said. My arm had ceased to ache. I had temporarily forgotten my shoulder.

"You ought to get someone to help you," Mummy told me. "What about Angela?"

Angela loved horses but for some unknown reason she wouldn't ride them.

"Do you think she'd like to?" I asked.

"Well, you know her better than I do. Why don't you ask her? She's not doing anything, is she?" Mummy replied.

"I should pay her of course," I said.

"Or I will if you like. I don't know what your finances are like," Mummy said.

"All right," I answered, remembering I had nine pounds in the bank—which wasn't much, but I had more coming in.

We had breakfast and then I telephoned Angela. She answered herself.

"Hullo, how are you?" she asked. "I hear you came a cropper yesterday."

I wondered why bad news spread so quickly. It was typical of our part of the world that Angela should know all about my accident the very next morning.

"I nearly rang up last night, but I thought you were probably in bed," she continued.

"Actually I expect I was at the hospital. I've got a broken collar bone," I explained.

"Oh dear, how awful! Does it hurt?"

"No, hardly at all, but I can't do much for a few days with my right arm; that's really why I rang up. Can you possibly come and help? I mean as a proper employee."

I waited anxiously for Angela's reply. I felt awkward about the paying part. Some people are peculiar about accepting money. I didn't know whether Angela would be. I was afraid she might be offended by the suggestion. I always accept money for jobs willingly, but some people don't. There was a pause and then she said, "But I'd love to. When shall I come?"

I said, "How marvellous," and began to look forward to the next few days. I thought it would be fun to do things with someone and I liked Angela.

"As soon as you like," I said.

"I don't see why you should pay me. I shall enjoy it," she told me.

"But I wouldn't have asked you if I hadn't intended it to be a business arrangement. I wouldn't have had the nerve," I said.

"Oh well, we can talk about it later," she replied. "I'll be over by the middle of the morning at the latest."

"You'll have lunch with us of course," I said.

We rang off. "It's settled; she's coming," I told my parents rushing into the kitchen. Daddy was just leaving. It had stopped raining. I could see Benedictine's wise head gazing into the yard. I felt much better now; I was sure everything would come right in the end.

"I'm so glad," Mummy said.

"Whacko," exclaimed Daddy. "No more mucking out for me. Not that I didn't enjoy it this morning."

I drank another cup of coffee, before I filled a bucket with warm water and antiseptic and bathed Fantasy's hock.

She was nearly sound and a very good patient.

She nuzzled me while I worked on her hock and blew down my neck. I sang for a time and then I started to think about Guy again. Had he really left? Why hadn't he said goodbye? I remembered that I had decided to write to him. I thought, I'll leave it till later, but I couldn't; it was on my mind; I had to do it right away. I went indoors and found my pen and a pad of paper. I sat down in a chair and tried to think. I didn't know how to begin.

I wrote, *Dear Guy* and saw us dancing together again. I tore off the sheet of paper and wrote, *My dear Guy*. I sucked the end of my pen. I wanted to tell him that Benedictine hadn't reared. I wanted Guy to know that I liked him.

I tore off the sheet of paper. *My dear Guy* seemed affected. I wrote,

Dear Guy,—l did enjoy dancing with you at the ball; also the champagne—thank you so much. I meant to thank you before I left but didn't get a chance. This is also to say goodbye, because I have a feeling you've probably left England by now.

It may surprise you to learn that Benedictine did NOT rear on Saturday; we merely fell into a stream.

I do so hope we'll meet again when you return,
Yours ever,
Jan.

I stood and looked at it for a long time when I had finished. I wasn't sure about the "Yours ever". I wanted to write "love", but did I know Guy well enough for that? I realised that there were too many "thank yous" and two "alsos". I thought of writing it again. Then I saw Angela arrive on a bicycle and hastily shoved it in an envelope and addressed it to:

Guy Maunder Esq.,
Littlewick Court,
near Summertown.

Angela was stroking Fantasy's nose when I appeared in the yard. She was wearing crimson slacks and a buff coloured high-necked jumper. She has dark hair and blue eyes.

My letter to Guy was in my pocket. I had put a stamp on it on the way out. I was anxious to post it before I changed my mind.

"What do you want me to do?" Angela asked.

"Well, there's tack or grooming, whichever you like. I haven't done either," I told her.

"Can I groom Fantasy?" she asked.

"Of course. The grooming things are in the saddle room. I've just got to go to the post."

I felt better when I had posted the letter. I felt that I wasn't letting grass grow under my feet; and presently I could start looking forward to a reply, and next time I would sign my letter, "love, Jan."

The work seemed twice as easy with Angela to

help. By lunch time nearly everything was done. Afterwards Angela and I washed up together; then we sat and talked and Angela looked at my ball dress. Later I rode Velveteen quietly for an hour in one hand. He was going much better now; soon he would be able to go home; presently I would be looking for new horses to school. I thought of all this as I rode. I felt that I needed an immediate success to boost my reputation. It would be awful if my stables were empty.

Angela was settling the horses for the night when I returned. We were finished by four o'clock.

I remember going to bed that night thinking, everything's going to be all right.

The next morning was sharp and there was a black frost. I rose early because I had decided to exercise Benedictine with hounds.

It was still dark when I gave Benedictine a small feed and put his tack on. Half an hour later dawn was spreading across the sky as I hacked towards the kennels. Benedictine was fresh after his day's rest, but Miss Peel's careful schooling had come back to him and I could ride him easily in one hand.

Tom was just letting hounds out. Jim, the whip, held the horses. There was a mist now, and they looked like a painting by Lionel Edwards in the murky morning light.

"Hullo, Miss. How are you?" Tom called as I

swung into the yard. He was wearing an ancient pink coat and a bowler hat, old boots, old breeches and a jersey. Jim was dressed much the same, except that he was younger so that his clothes were newer.

"Okay, except for a slightly wonky shoulder," I replied.

"What is it—a broken collar bone?" Tom asked.

"That's right," I said.

"Thought it looked like one on Saturday. I could see it by the way you walked," he told me.

He took it all as a matter of course. Broken bones were common in his profession. "Soon be all right, just rest it for a day or two," he advised.

Hounds were out now gambolling round the horses. It did my heart good to see them. I thought again, everything's going to be all right.

"We'll just go round the lanes," Tom said. "Keep your eyes skinned for foxes. There's plenty of scent this morning and we don't want to lose the pack."

We set off at a hound jog. Postmen were delivering mail, there was a rattle of bottles in the air. The day was really beginning.

Tom told me to go in front. "If that horse will go first," he said. His voice told me what he thought of Benedictine. I'll show him on Saturday, I thought. I'll jump everything but water, I'll ride with everything I've got. If they kill, I'll be first there. I had immense confidence in Benedictine. I still knew that he was the finest horse I had ever ridden.

We rode through a damp beechwood, where the trees dripped moisture on our heads and there were deep ruts where tractors had been. Hounds were full of life. Without looking round, I could feel them pressing on Benedictine's heels. They were just waiting for an excuse to go. We came to a lane and here it was easy to keep the pack back and I was able to relax.

"I must say he does go better with you," Tom said, looking at Benedictine. "But then those Stanmore girls are no good on a horse, scared stiff half the time they are."

"He's a lovely ride, and he hasn't reared once since I've had him," I replied.

I don't think Tom believed that, because he changed the subject. "What did you think of the ball?" he asked.

We discussed the Hunt Ball, turned into a road full of cars taking business men to work and trains. We had to hold hounds up in gateways several times because of traffic. I could feel their sense of frustration growing; they were longing for something to happen.

We followed another lane; came to open country and then what I had been dreading happened—a large jack hare got up right under the nose of the pack.

None of us had a chance, they had gone in a flash. Tom swore, Jim pushed his horse into a gallop. Tom started to yell at the top of his voice, "Ware Riot", and a host of other things I couldn't translate. Then he took his horn from between his buttons and blew. I went in pursuit of Jim. Benedictine didn't hesitate. It was as though it had always been his job to stop a pack of hounds fast disappearing in full cry.

Before us stretched miles of open country. Benedictine's stride felt strong beneath me; in spite of the awfulness of the situation, I felt an exhilarating wave of pure happiness. Guy and the Stanmores were forgotten as I crossed that landscape, only the pack mattered and Tom standing where I had left him blowing helplessly, endlessly in vain.

"We'll never catch them now," Jim cried, pushing his little chestnut faster, cracking his whip, beginning to yell remarks after the vanishing pack.

We breasted a hill; before us lay another open valley.

"We'll wait here," Jim said, drawing rein. "He's sure to run in a circle."

We sat on our panting horses. There was a faint breeze in our faces and a smell of stubble and new plough.

"That bay of yours can certainly go," Jim said.

"He's not mine," I replied, and suddenly wished

he was and, for the first time, I wondered what would happen when I proved that he was brilliant, a horse in a thousand, and far from vicious.

Jim was right. Already hounds were turning towards us. "Hares always run in a circle," he said.

We started to walk the horses. They were very hot. We didn't want them to catch cold. Tom had stopped blowing. In the distance a tractor was ploughing, turning green and gold stubble into rich brown earth. The sky was growing lighter each moment. It was a lovely day.

A moment later the hare flashed by. The pack was only a few yards behind. We stopped them, Jim cracking his whip. Behind us Tom started to blow.

"Thank Gawd," Jim said. "And no damage done."

He rated hounds as we rode back together. They looked sheepish and very, very guilty, but in their eyes a glint of excited happiness still gleamed.

Tom rated them when we reached him; they looked guiltier still; then we rode on together.

The gallop had done Benedictine good; his stride seemed even longer; he felt happy and interested, glad to be alive. Hounds were subdued for a time, and I remember thinking, this is a perfect day, and imagining Angela looking after the other horses and myself returning home to find food and water waiting for Benedictine, all the work done. I think the sun came out and I took off my gloves and thought how lucky I was to be riding with hounds while other girls sat in offices and typed or added up figures, served in shops or were still being educated.

I started to sing one of the songs from the "Water Gipsies." I relaxed, gave myself up to the beauty of the morning and to the swing of Benedictine's walk, and all the time there was tragedy waiting just round the corner only I couldn't see it.

10

I T happened so quickly; one minute we were riding whistling and singing, laughing and joking and the next moment we were in the midst of tragedy.

I was still leading when it happened; that was something which made it so much worse for me, because ever since I've had the feeling I might have stopped it happening. Tom and Jim say that's nonsense, they couldn't have done more themselves than I did. But I'm never sure.

We had crossed a main road and were riding across a common. Everything smelt of gorse and heather, pine needles and damp earth. The tracks were stony. Benedictine walked with care. I saw a stout woman and a little dog a hundred yards or more ahead and only thought, what a lovely morning for a walk; and then suddenly a new hound, Rambler, saw them. He was a long lean hound with shifty eyes and, without warning, he broke into full cry.

If I had been on the alert I think I could have stopped him, or at any rate the entire pack following him. But by the time I had collected my wits, they had all gone and Tom was screaming "Ware cur dog, hold up together there. Ware riot."

Then we were all galloping along the stony track with our hearts in our mouths. I think I prayed, let them see it's a dog. Don't let them kill it. I could see the woman hitting at hounds with a stick as they closed in; the entire pack sprang back except for Rambler—he went straight in to the kill. We were screaming now all three of us, and there was a high-pitched yap, which seemed to ring through the air. Then there was a ghastly silence and Rambler dropped the dog, and Tom muttered something I couldn't hear. We drew rein then. We all knew it was over. Rambler had killed the little dog.

The woman turned to face us. There were tears trickling down her cheeks. She was dressed in tweeds and sensible shoes. She was quite old. It was awful to see her cry. I don't think any of us knew what to say. Rambler was standing with a smile on his face, which Tom soon wiped off with his whip.

"That won't do any good now," the woman said.

It would have been easier if she's been angry. But she just stood and cried. And at her feet lay her little Corgi dead.

"I'm so sorry," I said, "so terribly sorry." But I knew it wouldn't do any good, nothing would do any good. The Corgi was dead and we couldn't bring him back to life.

"I wouldn't have had it happen for all the world," Tom said. "We've only had the dog a week. And he won't be with us after this afternoon."

I knew then that he meant to destroy Rambler, the penalty paid by a convicted cur dog hunter.

I thought, why did it have to happen? While the woman found a handkerchief and wiped her eyes.

"He was all I had," she said. "My husband's dead and my children have grown up and gone away. I can't think. I'm so sorry. I'm dazed I think. It's such a shock."

We'd all dismounted by this time. Tom looked at the little Corgi. Even in death he was very sweet. He was furry with little pointed stand-up ears and of course no tail. I think most of the pack had thought he was a fox right up to the last minute, except for Rambler. I think he knew he was a dog all the time.

"I expect you'd like us to take him home for you, Madam," Tom said. "Do you live near by?"

"Just a little bit further on, the thatched house with a lantern over the door," she told us. She was covering her face with her handkerchief. She didn't want us to know that she was still crying.

"I can't say any more. Yes, leave him at my house," she said.

"I'm so terribly sorry," I said again. But I don't think she heard. We mounted and rode on and she stood still in the middle of the path, her shoulders rocking.

None of us could speak for a time. I was crying again and there were tears in Tom's eyes, and Jim wouldn't look at either of us. The Corgi's last frightened yaps still rang in my ears. A gloom hung now over the blooming gorse, the heather and the pines. I've hated the common since that day.

We reached the house with the lantern hanging over the door. It was a large house for one old lady. I don't know what Tom said to the maid who opened the door. He came back wiping his hands on his breeches, mounted his horse and rode on in silence.

He only spoke once before we reached the kennels. "I've never liked that brute. I knew he was a rotter the first time I set eyes on him," he said, and I knew he meant Rambler.

We put hounds back in kennels and I said, "I'm sorry. I can't help thinking I might have stopped them." I looked away from Tom because there were tears welling in my eyes and wondered whether the Corgi's owner was home yet, and where she would bury him. I saw a little tomb in the garden with a cross over it.

"Put that right out of your head. You couldn't have done more than you did," Tom told me.

But somehow it was small comfort. I said goodbye and rode away and all the brightness seemed to have gone from the day.

My troubles seemed nothing in comparison with the little dog's dastardly death. I wondered why I had bothered so much about my reputation and Guy. It all seemed rather petty now, though of course Benedictine still mattered.

The beech woods were noble and very still. There didn't seem a breath of air anywhere. I longed for rain, for snow, something to help me forget what had happened. I didn't cry again. I walked Benedictine home with a sense of aching misery. I didn't notice my shoulder, nor how Benedictine went, though when he shied I shouted at him, which is something I never normally do to any horse.

I swung into the stable yard, looked for Angela and saw Guy. My heart gave a silly sort of leap and then stopped.

I said, "Oh hullo." I was surprised, but seeing him didn't give me the thrill it would have done a couple of hours earlier. I was pleased, but it just didn't seem to matter so much.

I said, "I thought you had gone," remembered

my letter and blushed. Angela was nowhere to be seen. I suppose she was trying to be tactful. Later she appeared from the direction of the house.

"I came to thank you for your very nice letter," Guy told me. He was wearing jodhs and a hacking jacket. I could see Prudence now in Benedictine's box. I didn't know what to say. Half of me was still on the common looking at the dead dog.

I dismounted and Guy said, "You've been exercising hounds, haven't you? How did you get on?"

I don't quite know what happened then. All my misery seemed to come to the surface. I think I gave a sort of gasp and then suddenly I was crying on Guy's shoulder, and he was patting my back as though I had a coughing fit and saying, "What's the matter, Jan? What is it?" I think I came near to loving him then, or perhaps I did. It's difficult to tell if you've never been in love before. He gave me a handkerchief and I blew my nose and wiped my eyes and said, "I'm sorry." I must have been hideous with my tear-stained face.

He said, "Poor Jan. I'm so sorry," and wiped a teardrop off my nose. I remember I felt like crying on his shoulder for ever.

Presently I started to explain and my misery increased as I told my story. Guy still had one arm round my shoulder and I remember how it suddenly hurt and I recollected that I had a broken collar bone.

When I had finished Guy said, "My God. How awful! It is something which only happens once in fifty years, but which huntsmen dread all their lives. Who was the woman?"

I said, "I don't know," and put Benedictine in the box which had been Domino's and wondered how long it would take me to forget.

I wished then that I was the sort of person who could think, *it was only a dog*. But I wasn't made like that, and anyway there was the old lady to consider.

Presently Angela appeared and I said, "Guy, please tell her what happened," because I was afraid she would start asking questions and I didn't want to talk about it any more.

Later we all had lunch together and Mummy found some beer for Guy. And I forgot that our house was shabby compared with Guy's and there weren't any servants. But even if I hadn't, I don't think it would have worried me. Suddenly I was past that stage in my life.

I felt like crying all through lunch and Angela and Guy made bright unconvincing conversation to each other. I think Mummy thought my collar bone was aching. She kept looking at me and presently she said, "I think you'd better rest after lunch, Jan. You look tired."

"I'm all right," I replied. "I'm going to take out Velveteen. He must be exercised."

"I'll take him," Guy said. "I'd love to."

I didn't want to rest. I would see Rambler killing the Corgi again, the old lady crying. I would go backwards and forwards over the incident until I was convinced that it had been all my fault.

"I don't think his owner would like it," I said. "Not that you aren't probably a better rider than me, but you know how funny people are."

Guy had finished. He was getting out his cigarettes. He offered one to Mummy.

"Why, am I likely to meet him or her? And if I do, can't I say I'm your groom?" he asked.

"They really can't object if they know you've got a broken collar bone," Mummy said.

"I should say not," Angela agreed.

I couldn't argue any more. I decided to take a book upstairs with me and try to read.

"Okay then. If you're sure you don't mind," I said, looking at Guy.

"I'd love to," Guy said.

We all washed up together. At least Angela and Guy did most of the work, while I watched. Somehow I'd never imagined Guy washing up, but really he was rather good at it.

"And now dear heart, please go to your bed," Guy

said, turning me round, forgetting my collar bone, pushing me into the hall.

I went upstairs with a book, but I couldn't read. I heard Velveteen's hoofs in the yard and Guy calling goodbye to Angela. I heard water running into a bucket and then Guy and Angela talking; their voices seemed to go on for ever. Then I think I slept. Some time much later I wakened to find Angela looking at me and saying. "Guy's just going. He's afraid you're asleep. Do you want to say goodbye?"

I went downstairs. Already I felt better. Guy was mounting Prudence in the yard. He waved.

"I had a lovely ride. Do you feel better?" he called.

"Much. When are you going?" I asked.

"Not quite yet. Probably not till the week-end. You know I was looking for you on Saturday. I didn't just go home," he told me.

I said, "How terribly nice of you. I had no idea. I thought perhaps you'd rushed home to pack."

"Far from it. When do we meet again?"

"On Saturday. I'm hunting."

"I shouldn't. Not Benedictine anyway," Guy said.

I thanked him for riding Velveteen.

"You're just changing the subject. What do your parents say?" he asked.

"I haven't spoken to them yet."

"Well I don't think they'll let you. Why don't you come on foot, you'll have lots of fun."

I wanted Guy to go now. I had decided to hunt. I didn't want to think about my decision any more.

When he had gone Angela said, "He's nice, isn't he?"

And I replied, "Yes," absent-mindedly, because I was thinking about Saturday. I was determined to hunt Benedictine. No one was going to stop me.

"He got on beautifully with Velveteen," Angela continued. "I should think he's wizard to dance with."

"Yes, he is," I said, wondering how I could ask my parents, what would they say? What would I do if they refused to let me go?

It was a lovely evening. In the west the sky was tinged with pink. The clouds were small and gay. The moon had risen.

I went round the horses with Angela. I watched her go to catch her bus; then I went indoors.

Daddy wasn't home yet. Mummy was making tea.

"I like Guy," she said.

I fetched the bread. "I'm so sorry about the dog," she continued. "It must have been horrible."

"Yes, it was awful. There's been nothing but accidents lately. It's the fourth I've been involved in: first Sonia, then Fantasy, then my toss, not that that was exactly an accident, then today. There seems to be a hoodoo on me."

I was beginning to think there was. Something had happened, I had never been so unlucky before.

"Everybody goes through bad phases. Life's like that," Mummy told me.

It was very warm in the sitting room. We drew the curtains and the firelight played on the walls. The morning seemed a long way off.

"I suppose my luck will change one day," I said. "I only wish it would hurry up."

"It's bound to," Mummy said.

My shoulder was aching now, not very much, but enough to be irritating, and though I tried to think of other things I saw the Corgi again and Rambler shaking him.

Mummy gave up trying to talk to me after a time and I sat and thought about the last two weeks and remembered that tomorrow was Tuesday and that I would be hunting on Saturday.

11

TUESDAY was one of those days when the telephone never stops ringing. First of all it was Miss Peel asking after Benedictine. She talked for ages. "He didn't rear, did he?" she began. I told her how he had fallen into the stream, how marvellously he had gone, how everyone misjudged him except us.

"And is it true about your collar bone? I'm so sorry. I can't help feeling that I'm partly responsible."

I remembered that hers was broken too.

"There's no need to, if it was anybody's fault it was mine. How's yours?" I asked.

"Nearly mended," she said.

A few minutes later she rang off. I had just reached the back door when it rang again; this time it was for Mummy.

Angela had arrived. Together we groomed the horses.

Then Mummy called.

"Telephone," she said.

It was the professor. His real name is Eastman—Professor Eastman. He said, "Good morning to you, Miss Craigson."

I wondered what he wanted. I said, "Good morning."

"And how is Fantasy?" he asked.

I started to tell him, but he interrupted. He didn't really want to know.

"I rang up because I have a free afternoon, and I would like to come over and see her," he told me.

I said, "That'll be lovely. If you tell me what time, I'll try to be in."

He said, "Early afternoon. Before three anyway."

He had put down the receiver before I had time to speak again. He didn't mean to be rude. Everyone knew he was like that.

Outside there was a piercing wind. It seemed to go through clothes and flesh to the marrow of one's bones. Bill Strawley was standing in the yard talking to Angela.

He called, "I see you have a helper," before he looked at Angela and said, "Six o'clock then."

I said, "What do you think of Fantasy?"

"Fine. Going along nicely. You'll be able to ride her tomorrow," he told me. "I've been looking at the Stanmores' bay. You've got plenty of quality there."

"I'm glad you think so," I said.

"What are they going to do with him eventually?" he asked. I felt a knot rise in my throat. I hated to remember that Benedictine wasn't mine and that he never would be. "I don't think they know themselves," I replied. But I started to wonder myself then. If he went well on Saturday, if I won my bet, they wouldn't have to send him to a sale without a warranty.

"He's worth a lot of money. I think I know of someone who might like him," Bill Strawley said.

The knot in my throat was growing larger. I thought, don't be silly, Jan, you never thought you could keep him. "Nothing can be settled till after Saturday," I said. "Everything is still in the lap of the gods."

Presently Bill Strawley drove away, but he had spoilt my morning. I was stupid enough to be already attached to Benedictine. I hated to think of him leaving. Since I had had him, I had realised just how mediocre most of my equine pupils were.

Angela's eyes were shining. "He's asked me out to dinner." For the first time I envied her her carefree life.

"I'm so glad. Is it tonight?" I asked.

"Yes, he's telephoning me at six to see how he's placed. I'm afraid I shall have to leave a little bit early," she told me.

"Don't worry about that," I said.

We saddled Velveteen. I had decided to school him. His jumping needed improving and he was due to go home on Monday. The wind had dried the ground in the paddock. It was bitterly cold; even with gloves my hands were freezing and, in a matter of minutes, my feet were like blocks of ice.

I rode him over cavaletti and gradually his stride lengthened and he began to move more freely. Presently I jumped him over my battered brush and my wall, which began life as a teak garden table. Angela appeared and stuck up a triple, a hogsback and a flimsy in and out.

Although she doesn't know much about jumping, she has often watched the experts on television and she was able to shout encouraging remarks and make suggestions. It was nice to have someone watching. I found my riding improving and Velveteen cleared the new jumps without any fuss at all.

"Jolly good," called Angela as I halted and patted Velveteen with my left hand.

"It'll be okay if he jumps like that when his owners come," I shouted.

I felt very happy now. I whistled as I rode back to the stable. I felt that my luck was changing at last. Mummy, Angela and I had elevenses together in the kitchen, before I mounted Benedictine and rode him to the paddock.

"Shout when you're ready and I'll come and stick up the jumps for you," Angela called after me.

I rode Benedictine very quietly for a long time. Then I started driving him into his bridle and felt his hocks come under. I was quite certain now that he would make a superb One Day Event horse; he had all the qualifications—balance, ability, pace, power and presence. I rode him over the cavaletti, did some work on two tracks, circled, before I called, "Okay, ready."

Angela and I stuck up the jumps together. I was so accustomed now to using my left hand mostly that I hardly noticed my right shoulder and collar bone. Angela held Benedictine while I mounted. It was still very cold, but I had ceased to notice it. I had taken off my gloves and now Angela looked at me and said, "Aren't you freezing?"

She was still lit up by Bill Strawley's invitation. She looked very attractive in a blue pullover and her crimson slacks.

"No, I'm all right," I said. "How about you?"

"Oh, I'm fine," she said.

Benedictine jumped marvellously. After

Velveteen, who was inclined to cat jump, his scope seemed immense. I felt as though he could jump anything. My three foot and three foot six jumps seemed like nothing at all.

"Gosh, he's marvellous. I can see now why you like him," Angela said.

"He would do for international competitions, wouldn't he?" I asked.

Angela hesitated for a moment before she said, "Yes, I think he would. Isn't it awful that he was nearly destroyed?"

"Ghastly," I agreed.

"What will the Stanmores do with him when they get him back?" Angela asked, and I felt the knot rising in my throat again.

"I don't know; sell him, I suppose," I replied.

"They ought to give him to you," Angela said.

"They won't do that," I said, and suddenly everything seemed pointless. I was schooling Benedictine, but for whom I didn't know. I was saving his reputation so that the Stanmores could make a good sale.

I said, "Let's go in," and turned Benedictine and rode across the paddock, through the gate and into the stable yard.

"I'm sorry if I said the wrong thing," apologised Angela.

"Of course you didn't. I'm just an escapist. I hate to think beyond today. It's lunch time anyway," I said.

My shoulder was aching again now. Mummy had cooked lunch. Angela and I dished it up.

"How did Benedictine go?" Mummy asked, and Angela said, "Beautifully, Mrs. Craigson. You ought to have been in the paddock this morning when Jan was jumping."

I could see that Mummy was upset. I guessed at once that she didn't like me jumping with my broken collar bone, but it was too late to do anything now.

"I wish you wouldn't jump, Jan," she said. "You know what the doctor said."

Angela said, "Oh dear, have I said the wrong thing?"

"I'm sorry. I didn't jump very high," I explained. "I only used my left hand."

"You're not going to hunt him on Saturday, are you?" Mummy asked.

There was an empty feeling in the pit of my stomach now. I had to hunt Benedictine on Saturday. I didn't know what to say. Angela and Mummy were both looking at me.

"I want to. I said I would," I replied.

"I don't think you should. Your shoulder matters more than a pound, and after all, he isn't your horse, Jan," Mummy said.

I knew that she was being reasonable. Any mother would have said the same. At any other time

I would have stayed at home on Saturday, but now there was so much at stake.

I said, "Oh dear, isn't life difficult?" I didn't know what else to say, I was simply playing for time.

"Can't you get someone else to ride him? What about Guy?" Mummy asked.

"He may be overseas by then," I replied.

"Well, I don't think you should hunt him," Mummy said again, and I looked beyond the Welsh dresser, hung with gay mugs, to the December day outside. I saw Saturday, hounds meeting, Tom and Jim, scarlet coats against the village green, shining horses, people chatting to one another, the Stanmores, Guy, Chris.

I thought of hounds drawing John Coltman's firs, the first canter, the wait at covert side. I couldn't think of anything to say. I suspect I was suddenly too sick to speak. I felt like running from the kitchen and burying my head in Benedictine's mane.

Angela said, "Oh dear," again.

I thought, the Stanmores will think I'm scared, they'll never believe me again if I don't hunt on Saturday.

I said, "I must go on Saturday," and looked across the kitchen at Mummy.

"Why don't you just go to the meet?" she asked. "I don't want to upset your plans, but you must be sensible." I hate arguing with Mummy. I said, "Yes, that's what I'd better do," and all the time I was thinking, I must hunt, I must, I must. It's not only for myself, I thought, but for Benedictine and Miss Peel. I can't let them down now.

Angela said, "Shall I clear away?" She sounded embarrassed, as though she feared a family row, which was silly because Mummy and I never quarrel. I remember we all cleared away and then there was stewed apples with meringue on top. I tried to be cheerful, but my gloom dominated the meal. There didn't seem any point in discussing Saturday further. I knew Daddy would agree with Mummy's decision. Angela talked rather obviously about a film she had seen and then she asked whether I thought she should wear a very new taffeta frock to go out with Bill Strawley or a slightly older wool one. I said it depended on the kind of invitation. Mummy told her the wool one for a cinema and the taffeta one if she was asked out to dinner. I said, "Why not ask him when he rings up?"

Angela gave a giggle and said, "Oh, I couldn't."

Then we heard the sound of a car turning into the stable yard and I gave a cry, and shrieked, "It's the professor."

Angela said, "I'll meet him and be your girl groom, while you comb your hair," and opened the back door and disappeared outside.

"You look quite tidy," Mummy told me. But all

the same, I hurried upstairs and improved my appearance. I returned to the kitchen and cleaned my shoes. Outside Angela and the professor seemed to be enjoying an animated conversation. I felt stupidly nervous, but when at last I ventured out, Professor Eastman greeted me with a hearty hand-shake. "Fantasy looks very well," he said.

I felt better then. "I'm so glad you think so," I said. I started to tell him about Fantasy being ridden next morning. But Angela had forestalled me. He said, "I know, I know. I'm very glad. I'm going to write you a cheque. I insist on paying for her keep during the last week."

I looked at Angela. I didn't know what to say. "I don't see why you should," I ventured at last.

His cheque book was already in his hand. "Four, five pounds? What is it?" he asked.

"Not five, that's the whole fee. A guinea will be heaps, honestly it will," I answered. I had always thought Professor Eastman disagreeable, now I felt embarrassed.

He wrote three pounds in a clear, neat hand. He said, "Miss Craigson, that's right, isn't it?"

"Yes, thank you. But you shouldn't pay and it's much too much."

He ignored my remark. He gave me the cheque.

"Her time's up at the end of the week, isn't it?" he asked.

"Yes, on Friday."

"I'd like you to keep her for another week," he said.

Presently he shook Angela and myself by the hand before driving away in his Standard saloon.

"What did you say to him?" I asked Angela.

"Nothing at all. I showed him Benedictine and told him about the Stanmores. I discussed young horses with him and I told him what Bill had said about Fantasy."

I noticed that Bill Strawley had become Bill. I said, "Is that all? Honestly?"

"Yes, of course it is," she said. "I think your luck's changing."

I said, "Don't mention luck. I've thought that before." I remembered the Corgi and that I wasn't to hunt on Saturday. I thought of my collar bone, and of Benedictine's fate which was in my hands. I said, "Everything's wrong whichever way you look at it, and there's no way out."

I crossed the yard and picked up a body brush and curry comb and started to groom Benedictine. Then Mummy called, "Telephone."

It was Chris. He sounded excited. "Hullo, is that Jan?" he cried.

"Yes, speaking. It's Chris, isn't it?" I asked. I couldn't imagine why he had rung up.

"I've just been talking to Captain Williams," he told me. "He's offered to referee on Saturday."

I leaned against the windowsill. The knot was back in my throat. I meant to say, "I'm not hunting." But the words wouldn't come.

"Don't you think it's a masterly stroke?" he asked.

"Very," I said. "No one can query his verdict."

I felt quite limp. I suppose my voice sounded flat, unenthusiastic, because Chris said, "What's the matter? You are still hunting, aren't you?"

There was a long pause which seemed to run into eternity. I tried to think of some way out, before I said, "Yes, of course I am." When I had uttered the words I wondered what had happened to me. Then I knew that I had to hunt on Saturday at any cost.

Chris said, "That's all right then. Aren't you pleased?"

"Yes, very. I think you're marvellous Chris," I replied, and wondered how I could hunt without my parents knowing and what they would say afterwards.

"How's your collar bone?" Chris asked.

"Nearly all right," I replied.

Outside I could hear Angela clanking buckets. I thought, other girls run away to Gretna Green and get married, it's not very awful to hunt when your mother's forbidden it.

"He's on your side you know," said Chris.

I was miles away. "Who?" I asked.

"Captain Williams of course," he said.

"Sorry, I'm afraid I'm stupid today," I told him.

"I expect you're doing too much," Chris said. "Try and rest a bit more. Let things slide."

"I am," I replied.

A second later he rang off. I stayed in the hall thinking. My life was certainly in a muddle, and I couldn't see how it could possibly improve. Whatever happened Benedictine would be sold, Guy would go overseas. It wasn't likely that Saturday would stop either happening. And there was nothing I could do except ignore Mummy's remarks about my hunting.

I left the hall and went out into the yard.

Angela was mixing feeds. I remembered that she was leaving early.

"It was Chris," I said. "He's asked Captain Williams to decide who wins the bet on Saturday."

"But you're not hunting," Angela exclaimed, putting down the bucket she had just picked up.

"Yes, I am," I said.

"But your mother ... ." she began and then stopped.

"I know, but I can't help it," I told her.

I helped feed the horses. Already evening had come. I watched Angela go. I settled the horses for the night. A mist lay across the yard; there was a feeling of frost in the air. I thought, everything's a muddle, you try to help one person and you hurt someone else. I listened to the horses munching, heard an owl hooting, and the distant sound of a train. I wished that I had a brother or sister, someone to discuss things with as I went indoors.

12

NOTHING exciting happened on Wednesday or Thursday.

On Friday there was a gale blowing and one of the elms in the paddock fell across the road and caused a commotion. We found it early in the morning and took out our large saw and sawed it in half. Daddy split it with a beetle and wedges; by nine o'clock most of the tree was back in the paddock.

No one had mentioned hunting again. Obviously my parents expected me to go to the meet and then return home.

Velveteen had returned to his owner. Fantasy was going better every day. Her rest seemed to have done her good. Benedictine was fresh, full of impulsion but easy to ride. Because he could never be mine, I tried not to enjoy schooling him too much.

Bill Strawley had taken Angela out for a drink in The Falcon. She had worn her wool dress. She expected another invitation any day and was forgetful; her mind seemed always far away, and she constantly saddled the wrong horse or gave Benedictine's feed to Fantasy or *vice versa*. And now the landscape seemed even bleaker than before, brussels sprouts drooped like people in the gardens, the fields were drab, the trees bare.

I rode Benedictine for two and a half hours on the Friday morning. On Thursday I had taken him exercising with hounds. Tom and Jim were still bowled over by the death of the Corgi. They had exercised hounds drearily on roads and, though the sun shone, it failed to dispel their gloom.

Guy had telephoned on Thursday evening.

"Hullo, is that Jan?" he had asked and then, "I go on Sunday night. You're coming to the meet on Saturday, aren't you?"

"Yes, that's right," I said. "I'm sorry you're leaving so soon."

"So am I. I wanted to ask you to come out with me tonight, but my aunt is coming and on Friday my parents are taking me out to dinner."

I thought, he wanted to ask me, and my spirits rose.

"We'll see each other on Saturday anyway," I said.

"Yes, but not for long," he told me.

I didn't contradict him. He would know soon enough that I intended to hunt all day.

"How's the collar bone?" he asked.

"Nearly all right I think."

"It can't be, it's much too soon," he said. "Anyway perhaps we can fix up something on Saturday. There's still Sunday," he said. He had a nice voice on the telephone, distinct and even and not too loud.

"That'll be lovely," I had replied and thought, everything will be over by then. I shall have won or lost. I shall have hunted. How shall I feel?

Presently he had said goodbye and we had rung off. The conversation had left me as dreamy as Angela for the rest of the day. Together we had muddled through the work and talked endlessly about Guy and Bill.

After lunch on Friday I schooled Fantasy, while Angela groomed Benedictine. The gale was still blowing and I remember I felt distrait and suddenly pessimistic.

Later we all had tea together in the kitchen and Mummy said, "I don't think you're going to miss much tomorrow, Jan; this gale looks like staying."

But she was wrong. On Saturday morning when I rose, needlessly early in the dark because I couldn't sleep, the wind had dropped; outside the air was almost muggy, the stable doors were damp to the touch, the garden paths woven with cobwebs. I tried not to think of my parents as I fetched the horses fresh water. I had dreamed that Mummy came to the meet and watched me ride to the first covert with tears streaming down her face. It was a dismal dream and I had awakened depressed with a sense of tragedy. Now I groomed Benedictine while gradually dawn came damp and grey. Presently Angela arrived and cried:

"What are you doing up at this time? I wanted you to stay in bed a nice long time, and now you've done everything." She was wearing a huge overcoat, which covered her ears.

"I couldn't sleep," I told her.

"You're becoming neurotic," she said. "Why don't you keep calm? You're not really going to hunt today, are you?"

"Yes, of course I am. I want you to tell my parents after eleven-thirty, please. I don't want them to get anxious," I told her.

I imagined her telling them. They would say, "Oh dear," and be upset for a long time. Then they would get used to the idea. That's what I hoped anyway.

The milkman called, "Good morning," as he left two bottles outside the back door. Men were bicycling along the road. It was an ordinary morning. I alone was besieged by doubt, guilt and a feeling of helplessness.

"Cheer up," Angela said, looking at my glum face. "I don't suppose your parents will mind much when the moment comes. I'll break it gently. And I'm sure Benedictine's going to behave beautifully, and I expect Guy will ask you out."

"He'll probably be furious. He doesn't approve of me hunting either," I said.

Angela came in for breakfast. We all ate boiled eggs, while outside the sky grew darker, and Daddy said, "It looks like rain."

"You'll be able to take a mac, won't you, Jan, since you aren't hunting?" Mummy said.

I nodded vaguely. I'm not a natural liar. I could never lie at school. Now I was hating breakfast.

I said, "I think I'll go and change if you don't mind."

I left my egg half eaten. Outside the weather-cock on the stable pointed north-west. I could see Benedictine looking over his box as I changed. His eyes were very large and kind. His neck looked long, and Angela had plaited his mane. If only I could buy him, I thought, combing my hair, finding my hat. I imagined him staying permanently, being mine, becoming my first horse. I stood and looked at him for a long time and thought, this is really goodbye.

Then I turned and went downstairs and offered to help with the washing up and when it was refused because of my collar bone, wandered outside and stood looking at the weather-cock without seeing it.

Some time later I mounted Benedictine and Angela said, "I'll tell them at half past eleven. Don't worry. Have a good day."

Mummy called, "We'll keep lunch hot for you."

I shouted, "Goodbye."

It was a long hack to the meet. The sky had cleared.

A soothing breeze ruffled the elms in the paddock. Benedictine walked into the road with a long easy stride.

"Good luck," Angela called after me.

I thought, it's begun. It's really Saturday, and I'm really on my way to the meet and Captain Williams is to decide who wins the bet. I pushed Benedictine into a hound jog and wondered whether all the Stanmore girls would be out. And what Guy would say when he saw I meant to hunt, and whether I would have to hack Benedictine back to Tumbling Fields when the day was over.

I came to Little Cross and turned right. A squirrel ran across the road. In the distance a cow bellowed and nearer a tractor was carting silage. Presently I heard hoofs behind us and a voice called, "Hullo. I thought I was never going to catch you up," and I turned to see Chris on his grey Daisybell.

"How are things?" he asked, as I halted and waited for him.

"Awful. I'm not supposed to be hunting at all," I told him. We rode on together.

"You mean your parents don't want you to?"

"Yes," I told him, looking ahead to where the road ran between banks topped by hedges, and on each side there were woods which ran gently upwards till they met the pale grey sky.

"Poor Jan. Do you think they'll mind a lot?" he asked.

"I don't know. Angela's going to tell them," I said. "Anyway, don't let's talk about it. How are you? Daisybell looks sweet with her mane plaited."

"Sheila did it. She worked with horses before she took up nursing," Chris told me.

"She's jolly good at it. Is she coming to the meet?" I asked.

"Yes. I should like you to get to know her. She's a sweet girl," Chris said.

We turned right by some cottages, and followed a lane which led between stubble fields, through a copse on to a main road.

"It's a long way to Hillman's Green," Chris said. "I don't usually hunt when the meet's so far away. I've come today in your honour."

I said, "Thank you. I'm flattered."

"I'm not the only one. I think there's going to be a record turn out."

I thought of them all slowly converging on the same spot, a host of horses, riders in scarlet, ratcatcher, black. Captain Williams on his big bay Sportsman, the Stanmores, Guy.

"I wish they weren't," I said.

"Don't worry, they're nearly all supporters," Chris told me.

I felt nervous now. Supposing I didn't succeed? Supposing I fell off again?

"This is the last time I ride for a bet. I think it's too miserable for words," I said.

"What about point to pointing?" he asked.

"No thank you. I'm not brave enough," I said.

We left the main road and followed a gravelled drive. "We're nearly there," Chris said.

We trotted together side by side. Benedictine's stride was much longer than Daisybell's and he kept trying to forge ahead. His head was very high; he sniffed the air; he seemed to know about the meet and that today we were hunting. I felt him grow pompous under me. I prayed, God let him be good.

We passed a large grey house and a park full of deer; then we came to a road, and to farm people hurrying on foot and bicycle, to bunches of chattering children, to women pushing prams, to the sound of hoofs on tarmac. "It can't be far now," Chris said.

Benedictine's stride grew more spirited. He arched his neck; he carried his tail like a banner.

I looked at Chris and said, "He knows he's hunting. I'm afraid he'll go up after all. He feels so excited."

My stomach felt suddenly empty. I felt like turning round and riding home. I was certain now of failure.

"Keep beside Daisybell. He'll be all right," Chris said. We came to the green and someone cried, "Here she comes." Benedictine was almost pacing now. There were already twenty or more horses assembled.

Chris looked at my face and said, "Keep calm. You'll only upset him if you get excited."

I said, "I am," and ran a hand along Benedictine's neck and murmured, "It's all right. It's all right. We're only going to hunt."

We halted for a moment, but Benedictine wouldn't stand, so we were forced to ride up and down the road and backwards and forwards across the green.

I saw the Stanmores arrive and one of them called, "Hullo Jan."

Benedictine was still behaving like a high school horse. Chris insisted that he looked "*Magnifique*," but to me he felt merely over-fresh, strung up, ready to do something silly.

Hounds came next with Jim and Tom keeping them well together, taking no chances today.

Tom called, "Hullo, you've brought him then."

"That's right," I said.

He was beginning to grow calmer. His stride was less elevated, his carriage more ordinary. Somewhere in the sky the sun was trying to break through the clouds.

"There should be a good scent today," Chris said. I didn't know whether to wish for a blank day or a good one. In his present state a "gone away" might drive Benedictine into a frenzy. But hanging about outside woods might be equally dangerous. But if we did run, once we were in the open I was certain he would go like a dream.

Sheila came and Chris abandoned me. There were no signs of Guy. A small girl on a Shetland said, "Good luck, Miss Craigson." I said, "Thank you." I didn't know who she was. I had never seen her before. I thought, *More people know Tom Fool than Tom Fool knows.*

She said, "He's a lovely horse. I think you're ever so brave."

"Yes, he's lovely. But I'm not really brave," I replied, and Benedictine started to run backwards and the empty feeling was back in my stomach, and my shoulder began to hurt.

"Hullo Jan. How is my dear Benedictine?" called Miss Peel, approaching, followed by a variety of dogs, small in a riding mackintosh, lithe and ageless.

"Marvellous, though a little over-fresh," I replied.

Captain Williams was riding along the road. He must have unboxed his horse somewhere further back. Hounds were growing impatient. A member of the press was taking photographs.

"This is the great day, isn't it? I'm sure he'll be all right. He's a pet really, aren't you my sweet?" said Miss Peel patting Benedictine. "I wish I could buy him back," she sighed.

"How much did you sell him for?" I asked.

"A hundred and I think he was cheap at that price whatever the Stanmores say." She was a small indignant figure now. She found a lump of sugar in her mackintosh pocket and gave it to Benedictine. The sun broke through the clouds and shone on the green, on the small cottages surrounding it, on the pond where ducks swam, on hounds and the hunt staff, on all of us.

"It's going to be a lovely day, Jan. I'm so glad. Don't worry, I know he'll be all right," Miss Peel said.

I saw Guy then and he cantered across to me on Prudence, and Benedictine started to dance and paw the ground.

"Sorry, have I excited him?" Guy asked.

"No, not really. He was excited before you came," I said.

"I thought I was going to be late. I wanted to see you before we moved off," he said. Benedictine was whirling all ways. I could see Small talking to Mrs. Stanmore. I heard Tom blowing a short toot on the horn. I said, "It's all right. I'm hunting," and thought, they're moving off at last.

Guy was in hunting clothes. He said, "No, not really? You must be mad."

"Perhaps I am," I said. "I expect I'm slowly getting worse and worse."

"Getting?" questioned Guy and now he smiled, showing a row of crooked teeth.

"We'd better go. They seem to be moving off," I said. Guy's smile had made me feel funny; my legs felt weak.

We trotted across the green after the rest of the field. "I suppose it'll be old Coltman's firs first," Guy said.

"I expect so."

Benedictine was behaving like a high school horse again. Guy called, "Morning, Sonia. Do you see Jan's out again to win her bet?"

Benedictine's neck grew more and more arched until it was like a bow waiting to spring; his hoofs hardly seemed to touch the ground. I wished I had cut his oats. I wished he would settle. I wished that everyone would stop looking at him.

"He seems jolly fresh. I don't envy you, Jan," Sonia said.

I knew I had to keep Benedictine together. If he became unbalanced or in front of his bit I would never be able to ride him with one hand.

"She's the bravest person I know," Guy said.

I wanted to contradict him. I said, "I'm not. I'm just foolhardy."

"I expect you're one of those lucky people without any nerves at all," Sonia called.

I thought, I wish I was, and wondered whether such people existed. "Do I look like one?" I asked Guy.

"No, I used to think you were, but you obviously aren't," he replied.

"I suppose you thought I was unbearably horsy, like the Stanmores do."

"I don't know. I don't think I thought much about you until the dance," he said.

Someone opened a gate and we entered a field. Benedictine gave a buck from sheer high spirits. I lost a stirrup and clutched his neck for a second before I regained my seat.

"Careful. I thought you were off," Guy said.

There was a man on a tall grey watching us. He wore the buttons of another hunt on his coat. He sat beautifully; he was obviously a horseman of experience.

A north-west wind blew in our faces as we cantered across the grass to the wood of firs. Hounds were in front. Jim was galloping on our right, hastening to watch a far corner before Tom put hounds in. I wondered whether Angela had told my parents yet that I was hunting. The early morning seemed a long time ago. How would she break the news? I wondered. And, more important, how would they take it? Looking at the firs, very dark against the lighter green of the grass, I thought they would understand.

"Cheer up, Jan," Guy said, looking at my face. "You'll probably be celebrating tonight."

"I don't think so," I replied, but I don't think he heard, because he started to talk to the man on the grey. I listened for a moment and then I heard the man say, "Yes, well actually I'm looking for a likely young horse for three-day eventing. I've searched three counties already, but now at last I've seen something I like."

I felt the knot rise in my throat again. I felt tears rising behind my eyes, and the futility of my unhappiness made me want to cry; for without asking I knew that the man on the grey had spotted Benedictine, that he was the horse that he liked after searching three counties, and that the better Benedictine went today the sooner he would be sold. I knew I should be glad—after all it would be a good home, but I wasn't or only half anyway. I rode away from Guy and the man before I could hear any more and stood alone among a crowd of strangers.

13

HOUNDS found nothing in the firs. Chris came across to where I stood and asked, "How goes it?"

"Okay," I said.

I felt defeated. I didn't care about the pound any more.

"You look so dismal," Chris remarked. "Does your collar bone ache?"

"No it isn't that," I said.

"It's your parents then," he suggested. "I don't suppose they'll mind."

"It's something silly," I told him.

"I bet it isn't. By the way did you see Sheila? I wanted to introduce you, but you were talking to Guy."

"We met at the ball," I reminded him. Benedictine was standing sensibly with his head up and his ears cocked.

Tom blew, *Long leave the covert*.

"Did you? They've drawn blank," Chris said.

Guy had stopped talking to the man on the grey. People were putting out their cigarettes, picking up their reins again. "I wonder where we'll go next?" I said.

Guy came across. He said, "Do you know he's Major Crossland? He's very taken with Benedictine. He seems to share your opinion and thinks he'll make a cross country horse."

I said, "Who?" though I knew. I thought of Benedictine going, walking into a horse box with his long strides. I saw myself looking at him for the last time, at his Roman nose, his large eyes, his depth of girth and terrific length of shoulder. I will never have another horse like him to school, I decided. I shall go on riding mediocre horses for the rest of my life. If I hadn't improved him and saved his reputation I might have borrowed some money and bought him for a song at a sale, as it is I've cut my own throat. He can never be mine.

"The man on the grey. You must have heard of Major Crossland," Guy said.

"Yes, of course I have," I replied.

"Why are you cross?" asked Guy.

"I'm not," I replied.

Hounds were out of the firs now, we were trotting towards a line of beech woods, touched with yellow by the pale December sun. I thought, don't let us quarrel. God, don't let us quarrel. If Benedictine goes and I lose Guy I shall have nothing left at all, I thought.

"I think he wants to buy him," Guy said.

I thought of the Stanmores selling Benedictine. How much they would ask—one hundred, two, three? They stood to make a profit I decided. Major Crossland was probably prepared to pay six or seven hundred, and if Benedictine went well today he would be worth every bit of that.

I think I was hating the Stanmores again as Tom put hounds into the firs and the field began to talk in undertones, to light their cigarettes again and wait. I thought, they'll probably pay me my schooling fee, ten guineas, and feel very generous, and I looked at Sonia sitting on a new horse they had on trial and thought, she'd wreck any horse in a week.

Guy must have been watching me, because he said, "She's really quite harmless and rather nice," and I felt myself blush.

"Am I so transparent?" I asked.

"You shouldn't hate people," Guy said.

Hounds found then. There was a sudden crash of music, a view holloa from further down the wood. I felt my heart leap. Benedictine came to life.

Another second and we were galloping down a muddy track with everybody else, ducking under branches, yelling, "Ware hole! Ware rut! Ware hound!" And nothing mattered now, but the cry of hounds, the thudding hoofs, the flying mud, the beauty and length of Benedictine's stride, the light ahead shining through the trees, which meant open country, the smell of damp wood, the wind, the reins between my fingers. We came to stubble and darker sky, to elms stirred by the wind, and to hounds running together with their heads down, a glorious patch of black, tan and white on the golden stubble.

Tom was galloping with them, doubling the horn. Benedictine increased his pace as we left the wood behind. His gallop had tremendous power, without effort we passed one horse after another until I found myself behind Captain Williams with Major Crossland on my right and Sonia on my left. And now we came to a hedge, long and low. It felt nothing to Benedictine. For one second we were in the air, before we were galloping on across rich new plough. I remembered how Velveteen had faltered on plough two weeks ago, how I had nearly turned back, how I had gone on to see Sonia and Benedictine topple over. I seemed to have come a long way since then. I felt centuries older. I was hardly the same person now. A labourer was opening a gate. We heard Tom call,

"Thank you, mate," and the man's gruff, "That's all right."

The gateway was poached. We slowed to a trot. Someone gave the man half a crown. Then we were galloping across grass towards a rail fence, and a road and a coal lorry parked near the verge.

Benedictine jumped the rail fence as though he had been hunting all his life. I heard someone cry, "Well done," and turned in my saddle to see Major Crossland galloping just behind.

We came to a stile set at an awkward angle in a wire fence. We took it slowly. We were leading the field now except for Captain Williams and Tom away on my right. We crossed a field of plough and now I was close on Sportsman's heels. Benedictine crossed the plough like grass. It felt nothing to him. He wasn't even blowing when we came to the end. I jumped off and opened a gate. He stood like a rock while I mounted. It was fast becoming the sort of hunt one dreams about. It didn't seem real at all. Major Crossland was about fifty yards behind now. Further back still were Guy, Chris and Sonia.

We came to a hill, long and steep. I could hear Sportsman blowing, but Benedictine took it in his stride. We jumped a flight of slip rails. Hounds weren't more than sixty yards in front. My collar bone didn't hurt at all. We crossed more plough, saw a tractor driver standing on his seat waving his arms.

Hounds swung left. We clambered over a bank into a lane, charged through a farmyard, jumped a gate and then we were on grass again.

The wind was behind us. In front a flock of sheep were huddled in a corner. In the distance someone was calling his dog. We jumped a hedge and then I discovered that I was passing Captain Williams, that his horse was sobbing for breath, that Benedictine still had plenty of wind left.

Hounds checked then; the sheep had foiled the line. The field caught up.

"Gosh Jan!" Sonia cried. "I should think you've earned your pound."

I saw Major Crossland coming towards me. Then, thank God, hounds found again, and we were all galloping madly across the grass to a spinney and a cut and laid hedge. Already Benedictine was outstripping the other horses. I thought, he would win the Grand National. He would win dozens of point to points, and then I was jumping a hedge on top of a bank and galloping on across stubble.

I opened a gate and we crossed a road. Hounds were running too fast now to give much tongue. The fields looked winterish, brown and grey and green. We came to a fir wood, with a well-cut ride down the centre and pheasant gates at each end. I could hear Tom blowing the horn, as Benedictine jumped the first of the gates, going a little flat, rapping it with the toe of a hoof.

It was dark in the wood, but already hounds had reached the other side. Benedictine jumped the second pheasant gate with care. Then we were in the open again and ahead of us was a flat stretch of country with hardly a fence to be seen.

I saw Mrs. Stanmore galloping towards us. I guessed that she had come out late hoping to meet hounds at the second covert. She had been lucky to find us, I decided. Hounds were very close together. They looked marvellous crossing the flat open fields; they looked like a drawing, a painting, like toy hounds on a toy landscape.

Mrs. Stanmore shouted something which I couldn't hear. I waved to her and galloped on. Grass turned to stubble, stubble to plough, plough to kale and here hounds checked again. I halted Benedictine. He was dripping with sweat, but he didn't feel tired. Tom arrived and started to cheer hounds. Then Captain Williams and the field arrived. They were all talking about Benedictine, Major Crossland most of all. I tried not to listen, but I heard someone say, "He's the Stanmores', Mrs. Stanmore's over there." I think I felt a little sick then.

Guy joined me and said, "How's your collar bone?" and at that moment it started to ache.

"Middling," I replied.

"Don't you think you've earned your pound?" he asked.

Hounds were now speaking again now. I had no intention of going home yet.

"No, I'm staying out till the bitter end." I remembered my parents. What were they thinking? Were they furious?

Then someone cried, "There he goes!" And out of the kale came a big dog fox and Tom started to blow the gone away and hounds started to throw their tongues again, and Guy cried,

"What a whopper!"

It was a moment before hounds were out of the kale, while we all waited impatiently, and horses pawed and jingled their bits and ran backwards into one another. But then they picked up the line with a tremendous burst of music and we were all galloping again and this time the fox was running into the wind, and Guy said, "He's making for his earth."

Benedictine felt as though he had just come out of the stable. He was longing to go. I stood in my stirrups. The wind rushed to meet us. I gave him his head and we surged past half a dozen other horses. I saw Mrs. Stanmore's surprised face, Sonia on her new chestnut, Chris who waved and cried, "He's going marvellously." All the world seemed mine.

There were acres of grass, more plough, before

we reached the cross-roads and a little signpost which said, "Beachcombe eight miles." I crossed one of the roads and galloped on. I was alone with Tom now and the cry of hounds.

"Your horse can go," Tom said.

"Where are we?" I asked.

"Right out of our own country," Tom replied. "That means we can't draw if we lose him?"

"Yes and no," Tom said.

We came at last to a beech wood and Tom said, "Just slip round to the far side, Jan, and you may see him come out."

It was a very large wood. We'll lose him here, I thought. I cantered round to the far side, and here it was very quiet. In the distance I could see a church steeple. I looked at my watch and saw that it was half past two.

Presently I could hear hounds hunting towards me, and Benedictine cocked his ears and gave a snort. I said, "Ssh," and my heart started to race, because I guessed that he had smelt the fox.

I heard Tom blow a short toot on his horn, I heard hounds plunging through undergrowth and then into view came the fox, large and dark and obviously hunted.

Benedictine quivered. We were close to the wood and the fox didn't see us; he slipped away towards the church steeple, while my heart leapt, and I thought, this is my day. I stood in my stirrups and hollered and presently Tom was blowing the gone away and galloping towards me with three-quarters of the pack. I could hear the field charging through the wood, then hounds picked up the line and were streaming away into open country again and Tom cried, "Well done," and we both galloped on together, our horses neck and neck.

We came at last to the church steeple and a little village where people were standing at their gates.

"They're only a couple of minutes ahead," an old man told us as we charged along the road, jumped a hurdle lodged on a bank and galloped on towards a hill topped with gorse.

"You'd better go on. Your horse is faster than mine," Tom said.

"Would you like to change?" I asked.

"No, go on. Don't wait," he replied.

I gave Benedictine his head and in a moment we were alone with hounds in front and nothing else.

I looked back and saw that the field were jumping the hurdle, then I settled down to ride steadily and with sense in pursuit of the running pack.

I thought hounds would stop on the hilltop, because it was the sort of place foxes choose for an earth. But when I reached the gorse, I saw them streaming across another valley with farms and houses and sheep and cows. A man came out of the gorse as I stood for a second to let Benedictine get his second wind. He was dressed in breeches and gaiters, a jacket and cap. "I headed him away from the earth," he told me.

"Thank you very much," I replied.

I galloped down the hill to the valley below, and to more fences and fields. I jumped a hedge, a tatty gate and a four-foot fence of slip rails. Benedictine was faltering now. He took off right under the hedge, only just cleared the gate, and rapped the slip rails. I thought, hounds must check soon, but they didn't look like it as they streamed across the unknown valley still in full cry.

I passed two hay ricks, narrowly avoided a harrow overgrown with weeds. I jumped into a sheep pen and out again.

I had lost sight of everyone now. I seemed to be galloping alone across the valley. And then at last hounds checked and riding forward I found them standing alone round a drain. I dismounted and prodded the drain with my whip and out of it came the fox; he missed the hounds by inches, and by the time I had mounted again they were all streaming away toward the river, gleaming dully through the greyness of the day.

I was glad that the fox had missed the pack as I galloped on. I wanted him to get to ground now. He had given us a tremendous run. He deserved to save his brush. Benedictine was very tired. He stumbled over hillocks as we crossed a rough field smelling of thyme and wild rosemary. I pulled him up and let him blow before I put him at our next jump, some rickety rails in a corner. And now we were galloping across river fields, smelling of damp and mud and wet reed. I thought, supposing he crosses? Shall I swim the river? I wondered whether I could swim with my wonky collar bone? I didn't want to drown.

But now hounds were turning right towards an osier bed, and I had to stop to open a gate, and by the time I had mounted again they had disappeared.

I cantered on towards the osier bed, pushed Benedictine through a muddy stream and remembered the last time I had hunted by the river.

I turned in my saddle and saw that the fields behind me were still empty, before I entered the osier bed.

I found hounds baying round an earth. They had that disappointed look people have when they've missed a bus. I was sorry for them, but glad that the fox had got safely to ground.

I made a few encouraging remarks to hounds. Except for their voices it was very quiet in the osier bed. And suddenly evening seemed to have come. I dismounted and loosened Benedictine's girths. His head dropped. He looked almost finished.

I didn't know what to do. Hounds were losing interest in the earth. I suppose I'd better go back and try to find someone, I decided. I called to hounds, tried to sound like Tom, without succeeding. I led Benedictine back through the osiers. My legs were aching and so was my shoulder, but I think I felt very happy until I remembered Major Crossland and his quest for a three-day event horse. I looked at Benedictine and thought, you're as good as sold, and tried not to mind as I started to walk back across the river meadows.

14

IT was very quiet. Somewhere far away a church clock chimed the hour. Benedictine walked slowly, his head down. Hounds followed me solely because there was no one else. I went back over the last few weeks as I walked. I remembered seeing Benedictine at the meet, at Little Cross, the accident, being alone with Guy for the first time. I recollected my telephone conversation with Miss Peel, my visit to the Stanmores and my sense of inferiority. It all seemed to have happened a very long time ago. I remembered breaking my collar bone, trying to convince the Stanmores that I was telling the truth. Everything seemed over now. I had won my bet. Benedictine would be sold. My life would return to normal. The sky was dull overhead and it suited my mood. Guy was going. Benedictine was going. Life didn't seem to have much point any more. I had reached the heights, gazed at a new world and now I had to return to normal.

I turned and counted hounds. There were twelve couple. I guessed that some were lost. The Flintshire usually take out about fifteen. I wondered where the field was. Would it ever find us trudging alone across the wet river meadows?

I remembered the ball, writing to Guy. How I had fussed! And now somehow it all seemed rather futile.

We came to a gate and to a lane which led to the church which had chimed the hour. I mounted Benedictine and hounds smiled at me; they seemed pleased to see me on a horse again.

I rode on, and though Benedictine was tired, he still walked with a long swinging stride. I thought, this may be our last ride together and leaned forward and patted his neck which felt harsh now that the sweat had dried.

I remembered my parents waiting at home. Were they anxious? I wondered, coming to the church, turning left along a winding road, hoping that it would lead me home. No one seemed about. It was as though Benedictine and I and hounds were the only living things in the whole world. And then suddenly I heard the horn and hounds stopped and gazed into the distance with pricked ears and Benedictine's head came up.

I cried, "Hold up there," to the pack, because I didn't want to lose them, and pushed Benedictine into a trot. I had a funny feeling in my tummy now and it felt quite empty. Quite suddenly I didn't want to meet the Stanmores. I wanted to ride home alone with my own thoughts. And then I heard the horn again, much nearer this time. Tom was blowing, *Home* and *Long leave the covert*. And I thought, I suppose I may as well collect a pound. I rode on with a knot in my throat which kept rising. Benedictine trotted with his head up and his ears pricked. Hounds were inclined to rush on now that they had heard the horn, and my shoulder had started to ache again.

I came to another road and I could hear hoofs quite clearly now and I had to call the pack together again. It was very nearly dark, and there was rain in the air. I halted and waited with hounds clustered round Benedictine; and presently Tom came into view still blowing the horn.

His pink coat looked marvellous in the gathering dusk and somehow suddenly nothing seemed quite real. It was all too like a drawing, the damp air, tired hounds, a tired horse, a pink coat coming along the road.

"Hullo. You've got them then?" Tom called. The

field was behind him, Captain Williams, Guy, Chris, the Stanmores, a host of strangers. Only Major Crossland seemed missing.

"They ran him to ground in some osiers," I said.

"Your bay went all right," Tom said.

Captain Williams was smiling. "You've certainly won your pound," he told me.

I didn't care about the pound now. I didn't even want it.

But Captain Williams was waiting for an answer.

"Thank you very much," I replied.

Tom was counting hounds. He had brought three couple with him along the road. "All on," he said.

Chris and Guy came towards me together.

"Hullo," Guy called. "We thought we were never going to see you again."

"The Stanmores will certainly have to cough up now," Chris said.

I didn't care about the Stanmores any more. I didn't even hate them now. I felt very miserable as I looked at Benedictine's long ears. I thought, it's all over now. Tom blew the horn again and then we all turned for home.

"The Stanmores are going to sell Benedictine to Major Crossland," Chris told me.

The knot seemed twice as large in my throat. I was afraid I was going to cry. I thought, don't be a fool, Jan, from the moment you saw Major Cross-land you knew this would happen. But it didn't make things any better.

I said, "Are they?" and there was a choke in my voice, and I turned away and looked across the dusky fields where a line of trees met the dark sky.

"She's tired," Guy said.

The Stanmores were talking together at the back. They hadn't spoken to me yet. "It'll be a good home anyway," Guy said.

"Yes, very," I agreed.

Captain Williams had halted his horse. Now he rode alongside me. "Tell me exactly what happened. Where did he go to ground?" he asked.

His pink coat was muddy, his mahogany topped boots muddier still.

I started to tell him about the last part of the run. He wanted exact details. "Which field? Which osier bed? Which church?" he asked.

I didn't know. I had never been in those river meadows before, it was my first glimpse of the church. My answers were very unsatisfactory. I could only say, "Long fields with lots of willows. The osier bed had a stream on the outside. The church had a spiky steeple." We came to a cross-roads and turned left. We were a long way from home.

When Captain Williams had finished Guy started to ask questions of a different variety.

"What about tomorrow?" he asked. "Can you manage anything?"

I remembered that it was his last day. He looked a little tired and muddy, and his breeches were no longer white.

"Yes, I'd love to. Can you ring up when I'm home?" I asked.

"No, let's fix it now," he said.

"Yes," I said, trying to pull myself together, remembering that tomorrow would be Sunday.

"The films are bound to be awful," I said.

I couldn't visualise tomorrow. There was still the long hack home, my parents to face, Benedictine to put away. "I wasn't thinking about films," Guy said.

I could hear Sonia talking now. Someone said, "Three hundred guineas." I felt suddenly sick.

"You'll need cheering up," Guy said, suddenly kind. There were woods now on each side of us, large and dark. The clip clop of hoofs made me think of highwaymen.

"Oh, I'm all right," I said.

"What about dinner?" Guy asked.

"Lovely," I said. "Thank you so much."

At last we came to familiar land, to a cottage near a bridge, to more cross-roads and to a signpost which said Summertown eight miles. Several members of the field disappeared after calling, "Good night, Master. Thanks for the day."

After they had gone the night seemed darker still. Guy rode beside me. Sometimes our shoulders brushed. From time to time I could feel his eyes on my face. Having him so near did something to the marrow of my bones.

Presently he said, "Will you write to me while I'm away?" and I turned and met his eyes. "Yes, every day if you like."

"That's a promise," he said.

The Stanmores were still conferring together.

"It sounds as though they're holding a board meeting, doesn't it?" Guy asked.

I laughed. I couldn't be miserable with Guy beside me. Everything he said was like a dream coming true.

"Yes, terribly. I wonder what they're talking about," I said.

We came to more cross-roads and Chris came forward to say goodnight.

"You've worked marvels on that horse, Jan," he told me. "You must be a witch."

"Just horse sense, isn't it, Jan?" Guy asked.

"Luck mostly," I said.

Chris disappeared and with him three other riders. There weren't many of us left now.

"Have you got your pound yet?" Captain Williams asked.

"Not yet," I said.

We were riding along a big road now. Tom sent Guy and me on ahead to slow the traffic. Night had really come. Cars flashed past to and fro from London. Lorries passed more slowly. The better drivers dipped their lights when they saw hounds, others rushed on regardless.

"I wish I wasn't going. Somehow I've met you too late," Guy said.

"A year isn't very long," I answered, thinking of him coming home.

"But you may like someone else," he told me.

I couldn't imagine liking any one more than Guy. No one else had given me a funny feeling in my bones, nor made my heart leap like Guy. "I don't think so," I replied.

We heard the Stanmores say goodnight.

"But they haven't given you your pound," Guy said.

"Perhaps they've forgotten," I suggested. I started to think about Benedictine again then.

I thought of my stable without him. I wondered why the Stanmores hadn't spoken to me. I decided that they felt embarrassed. I imagined them making a deal with Major Crossland and all the time there was the knot rising in my throat again and tears pricking at the back of my eyes.

Guy must have been watching me, because he said, "What's the matter, Jan?"

I said, "I was thinking about Benedictine going, that was all," and remembered crying on Guy's shoulder.

"It's a shame. But he'll have a good home if he goes to Major Crossland. You'll be able to follow him in *Horse and Hound* and feel you've got a stake in him."

But I didn't care about having a stake in Benedictine. If anyone was to ride him in One Day Events I wanted it to be me. But asking for that was like crying for the moon, I decided. If only the Stanmores had given me the pound I could have been miserable in peace. As it was they had left an outlet for hope. Perhaps they had turned down Major Crossland's offer. What then? I asked.

A few more minutes and hounds and the Master had left us. Tom called, "Well done, Jan. You beat us all today." The Master said, "I'm sending you a young horse to school." Then there were only myself and Guy hacking together along an empty road. We didn't talk for a time. Once a squirrel ran in front of us; somewhere far away a cow was bellowing for her calf.

"Have a cigarette," said Guy at last.

He lit one for himself, and found some chocolate in his pocket, which he gave to me. Our horses walked peacefully side by side like old friends. Benedictine felt very tired.

"I'm going to walk," I said.

"I will too then," Guy replied.

We dismounted and banged against one another. We laughed and walked on together. In a tree an owl hooted. It was an eerie night I suppose, but to us though it was cold it seemed friendly.

"I'll borrow the car and pick you up in it tomorrow," Guy said. "Can you manage six?"

"Yes easily," I said, thinking what shall I wear?

"We'll be able to go to lots of dances and ride together when I come back," he said.

Everything seemed so easy now that we knew we cared for one another. It was maddening to think that a year must pass before we should dance or ride together again. We've wasted so much time, I thought.

"It'll be something to look forward to," Guy said.

"Yes. *Better to travel hopefully than to arrive*," I quoted.

"That's so pessimistic," Guy said.

And now suddenly we had come to our different ways.

"If Prudence wasn't tired, I'd see you home," Guy said.

"I shall be all right. Tomorrow at six then?" I replied. There was a tiresome lump rising in my throat again. I didn't want to say goodbye to Guy. He took my face in his two hands and kissed me. "Yes, tomorrow at six," he said.

I mounted in a daze. I said, "That'll be lovely," and then I was riding away along the road to home, with the feeling of Guy's kiss on my lips. I thought, he kissed me, and I felt suddenly warm and secure and quite stupidly happy.

I was still in a daze when I reached the stable yard, saw Angela waiting for me in the saddle room and the lights from the house shining across the road.

I remembered then that I shouldn't have hunted. That by rights I should have been home by lunch time. I waved to Angela and rode into the yard.

15

"YOU'RE terribly late," Angela said as I dismounted.

"I know, but he went like a dream. I've certainly won my pound. What did my parents say?"

"Lots of things," replied Angela darkly.

"Don't be a beast. Were they furious?" I asked.

"No, not really," she said.

"Who was the angriest?" I asked, putting Benedictine into his box.

"Not much to choose between them," Angela replied. I took off Benedictine's tack.

"Honestly, what did they say?" I asked. And then I heard the back door open and I saw my parents silhouetted in the doorway.

"Is that you, Jan?" Daddy called.

"Yes. I hope you haven't been anxious," I shouted. I wanted to be tactful, diplomatic, but that was all I could think of to say.

I could hear them coming along the garden path as I bolted the loose box door.

"We think you're very wicked," Mummy said.

"How's the shoulder?" asked Daddy.

They aren't angry, I thought.

"Quite all right. I'm sorry to be so late," I replied.

"We were coming to look for you. Then Mrs. Stanmore rang up," Daddy said. "Apparently you were a success on that unreliable bay."

At the mention of Mrs. Stanmore my heart had started to race.

"What did she want? Why did she ring up?" I cried.

"Don't ask me," Mummy said.

"She's going to ring up at half past eight," Daddy told me.

"But it's hours till then," I cried. I thought, she's ringing up to tell me that Benedictine's sold. I felt miserable again now. "Didn't she say anything else?"

"Nothing except that you were all right and that the horse went marvellously," Daddy said.

I said good night to Angela and followed my parents indoors.

"You shouldn't have gone," Mummy said. "It won't have done your shoulder any good."

I knew she was right. Now that I was still it had started to ache like mad. "We rang up the doctor and he was furious," she said.

I slumped down in a chair. "I'm awfully sorry. I had to go for Benedictine and Miss Peel."

Mummy poured me out some tea. The kitchen was warm. I felt large and clumsy in my hunting clothes.

"The water's hot if you want a bath," Mummy said. Then the telephone bell rang. "That's Mrs, Stanmore," I cried, leaping to my feet.

I glanced at the clock on the chimneypiece. It was seven o'clock. I dashed into the hall.

But when I picked up the receiver it was Miss Peel I heard speaking.

"Hullo, is that Jan?" she asked, while I felt a wave of disappointment sweep over me.

"Yes, speaking," I replied.

"I heard my dear Benedictine went marvellously. Honestly I can't thank you enough, ducky," she said.

"It's all right. I've enjoyed having him," I replied.

"I can't tell you how much it means to me," she said.

"I think he's sold or going to be sold to Major Crossland, you know, the cross country man," I told her.

"I've heard that. It's marvellous, isn't it?" she asked.

The lump was back in my throat.

"Yes, marvellous," I agreed.

If she's heard, he must really be sold. I decided I didn't care if Mrs. Stanmore rang up or not now.

"I want to give you something," Miss Peel said.

"Oh please don't bother. I've enjoyed having him. He's taught me an awful lot," I replied. "Anyway, look how much you've done for me in the past."

"Nonsense," she replied.

She continued talking in the same vein for a long time.

When I returned to the kitchen my tea was cold.

"That was Miss Peel," I told my parents.

I wanted to wash up and help get supper, but when I had finished tea, Mummy told me to hurry upstairs and have my bath. I undressed slowly. My shoulder felt all wrong and it looked funny too. Tomorrow I would have to have it reset I guessed. The doctor would be furious, but perhaps since it was Sunday I should have a strange one who wouldn't know anything about it. Everything would be all right then, I decided, seeing the hospital again in my imagination.

I stayed in the bath for ages. When I returned downstairs supper was ready.

"How does your shoulder feel now?" Daddy asked.

"All right," I said.

"It looks awful to me," he told me.

I didn't feel like a lot of supper. I had eaten too much tea.

"You look all in," Mummy said.

"We'll run you into the hospital to see that everything is all right tomorrow," Daddy told me.

"Can it be in the morning, please? I'm going out with Guy. It's his last evening," I said.

"Yes, of course," Daddy said.

I clung to the thought of seeing Guy on the morrow. I tried not to think of Benedictine. Then the telephone rang again.

"I'll go," I said.

This time I didn't hurry. I felt sure I knew exactly what Mrs. Stanmore had to say. I picked up the receiver and said, "Jan Craigson speaking," but though I felt calm I couldn't stop my heart racing.

"It's Mrs. Stanmore. Did you get back all right?" she asked.

I thought, she's leading up to it. I felt a little sick. "Yes, thank you," I replied.

"The bay certainly went well. You were quite right about him," she told me.

"He's a nice horse," I said. I wished that she would say what she had to say. I wanted to know how soon Benedictine was to go, and whether Major Crossland had really bought him.

"He's very fast too," I said.

"Of course you're a professional, so naturally you ride better than Sonia. My girls ride just for fun," she told me.

"Sometimes I wish I wasn't. I should love to have just one of my own," I said.

"Are you sure? I mean, could you afford to keep one?" she asked.

"Yes, yes, I know I could," I replied and suddenly my hand felt sticky against the telephone receiver. Why was she asking? What did it mean? "Particularly if the horse was talented. I mean then in time the prize money would help," I added.

"We were wondering about you. My husband and I feel you've done a wonderful job with Benedictine, so do the girls," she said.

I could feel my heart hammering against my ribs now. I thought, this isn't true. Benedictine's sold to Major Crossland.

"We thought you might like him. We think you deserve to have him. You see if you hadn't taken him, we would probably have sent him to the kennels," she said.

"Do you really mean it?" I asked, and suddenly I was crying with relief and remembering all the horrible things I had thought about the Stanmores and how beastly I had been.

"I should love to have him. But what about Major

Crossland?" I asked. I felt that they were throwing away at least three hundred guineas.

"We'd rather you had him," she said.

I didn't know how to thank her. I kept saying, "Are you sure? Wouldn't you rather sell him?"

Until she said, "Listen, Jan, we've made up our minds. That's the way we want it to be, so stop worrying."

I said, "I will. But thank you so much. I just expected a pound, that was all."

"Well, you won't get a pound now, only Benedictine," she told me.

I began to laugh then. I felt quite stupidly happy. She rang off and I stood by the telephone in a daze. I wasn't laughing or crying, but I still couldn't believe that it was true.

I walked into the kitchen and kissed both my parents. "Guess what? I've been given Benedictine," I cried. I started to explain and then Daddy fetched a bottle of sherry and said, "This calls for a celebration, I think."

We all drank to Benedictine and then we stood and discussed the Stanmores and how terribly I had misjudged them.

My collar bone had stopped hurting for the moment. I felt like singing, charging out into the night and shrieking to the world, "Benedictine belongs to me. He's mine, mine, mine, mine."

"I'm going to ring up Guy," I cried, suddenly hurrying into the cold hall, picking up the receiver, dialling the number of Littlewick Court.

A strange voice answered. "Can I speak to Guy?" I asked.

"Can you leave a message? They're in the dining-room," the voice explained.

I felt I must speak to Guy. He had to know. "No. It's urgent," I replied.

I could hear him coming towards the telephone. He picked up the receiver.

"It's Jan," I cried. "Sorry to drag you from your dinner ... I've been given Benedictine. I had to tell you."

"But how wonderful. Not really?" he asked.

"Yes honestly. Isn't it marvellous? I still can't believe it," I cried.

"Simply marvellous. How nice of the Stanmores. I am glad."

We talked about Benedictine and then Guy said, "It's still all right about tomorrow isn't it?"

I said that it was, and after that we talked for ages, until Daddy appeared and started to murmur about a call he had to make.

I hung up the receiver very slowly. I thought of Guy returning to his dinner. I thought, on Monday he will be gone, but it doesn't matter too much because we'll write and in a year he'll be home again. I thought of all I might do in that year. I would improve Benedictine tremendously, I would improve myself. I think I felt very happy as I returned to the kitchen.

"I must say goodnight to Benedictine," I told my parents.

"Don't be long. The sooner you're in bed the better," Daddy said.

"Don't lift anything," Mummy told me.

There was a moon now and a million stars. Benedictine was looking over his loose box; his large kind eyes looked full of wisdom.

I gave him a piece of bread which I found in my pocket. I patted his long bay neck. I thought, supposing I had refused to ride him, all this would never have happened. I would still be plain horsy Jan who schooled other people's horses. I remembered that someone had told me once that what you put into life came back to you again.

All I had done was to take Benedictine to please Miss Peel and now he was mine, and I was Guy's girl-friend. As I walked indoors it seemed that all my dreams had come true.

CHRISTINE PULLEIN-THOMPSON: A BIOGRAPHY

Christine Pullein-Thompson (1925–2005) was one of the three Pullein-Thompson sisters, authors who bestrode the pony book world in its prime. Their mother, Joanna Cannan, wrote some of the earliest books in the genre with her Jean series, and her daughters picked up the theme and ran with it. Brought up in bohemian surroundings, they lived the lives they wrote about.

Twins Christine and Diana were born in 1925, two years after their elder sister, Josephine. The girls had relatively little to do with ponies until the family moved from Wimbledon to The Grove, a country house in Oxfordshire. Once there, their parents decided they should have a horse.

Countess was not an immediate success: both parents were used to having grooms, and the practicalities of putting a bridle on the aged polo pony themselves caused some difficulty. However, the children were unfazed, and the family horse soon became their province. They read the equestrian works of Henry Wynmalen out loud to each other, trying to improve, and they became competent enough to take on the schooling of other people's horses, with local horse dealer Mr Sworder sending ponies to live at The Grove to be worked on.

The girls' schooling was patchy. They went, briefly, to Wychwood School. In 1938, after a polio outbreak struck Oxford, where Wychwood was based, the Pullein-Thompsons were removed from the school. When they returned, they were way behind their peers, and their parents used the girls' low marks as a reason for removing them permanently. They were then educated at home, so had every afternoon free to ride.

By 1939 and the outbreak of the Second World War, the girls had several ponies, but, with the blockades of shipping, supplies of food for them became scarce and ever more expensive. To raise money to keep them, the girls started The Grove Riding School. It flourished, as did the girls: Christine was told she was the kindest instructor.

Christine and Diana, then sixteen, were left in charge of the riding school when Josephine went to do war work at the remount depot in Melton Mowbray, where horses intended for use in the war were trained.

After the war they opened a second riding school at Wolvercote, and by the 1950s were operating two stables with 42 horses. Diana's career with horses ended when she developed TB; she then went to London and worked with a literary agent. Christine went to America in 1952 to work as a professional rider.

In 1954, Christine married Julian Popescu, settling in Oxfordshire, where they went on to have four children: Philip, Charlotte, Mark and Lucy, all members of the Pony Club. The family moved to Suffolk in the 1970s, when Christine was eventually forced to give up riding because of back problems. This did not stop her writing, or being concerned with making life better for other people. She set up a bridleways group and became chairman of the local parish council, and was a member of the British section of Pen. She was also much involved with the charity Riding for the Disabled, helping to found two of its branches.

Christine, like her sisters, wrote throughout her life, continuing a habit that had started when they were small. Writing was part of everyday life: the children produced their own family magazine, *The Grove*.

Their first articles, and their first book, were written by all three. Articles and short stories in *Riding* magazine were followed by a novel, *It Began with Picotee*. Although not published until 1946, it was finished by the spring of 1942, when Josephine was nineteen and the twins seventeen. The story, written during the ponies' rest days, 'emerged slowly as we argued over every word,' and 'giggled a lot'.

Christine's first solo novel was *We Rode to the Sea* (1948), very different from the first solo books her sisters produced. Josephine's *Six Ponies* (1946) and Diana's *I Wanted a Pony* (1946) were domestic riding adventures; Christine wrote about Scotland, adventure and escaped prisoners. She went on to write titles more firmly based in the horsy life she knew, like her hunting series, the Chill Valley Hounds, but continued to embrace adventure, with titles like *Riders from Afar* (1954) and *Stolen Ponies* (1957).

During the 1960s, she branched out, with stories aimed at younger readers in which there was not a pony in sight, but in the 1970s she returned, with the Phantom Horse and Black Pony Inn series, to stories based firmly on ponies and the children who loved them.

By the end of her career, Christine had produced

pony stories covering pretty well every aspect of the genre, from tales of a wild horse to holiday adventure, rescue stories, hunting, and, of course, classic pony stories.

She was the most prolific of the Pullein-Thompson sisters by far, with her bibliography numbering over a hundred titles. The sheer volume of Christine's books, allied to the number of different story types she tried, can sometimes obscure her real achievements in the pony book genre. Strong narrative frameworks showed Christine at her best: both *The Horse Sale* (1960) and *A Day to Go Hunting* (1956) take a situation (a horse sale and a day's hunt respectively) and take a thoroughly satisfying look at the way in which a widely differing set of characters react to it.

Her books have been read, and continue to be read, by generations of pony-mad children. All the Pullein-Thompson books ring with authenticity. The reader is never in any doubt that these are realistic ponies, in situations they might well meet as a rider, and with people familiar to anyone who rides. Like her sisters, Christine allied solid instruction to an involving story, and she never lost her determination to improve the lot of the horse. She wrote, in their joint autobiography, *Fair Girls and Grey Horses* (1996):

I have been told that our books changed the way people treated horses. I hope so. Certainly we considered horses individuals and friends rather than animals to be exploited.

Jane Badger

PUBLISHING HISTORY

The Impossible Horse was the only fiction title Christine Pullein-Thompson wrote under her pseudonym, Christine Keir. This was possibly because the book's content was aimed at more mature readers than her usual stories of children and their ponies. In *The Impossible Horse,* the heroine has left school, has started her career and is contemplating a relationship. There is also a particularly grim hunting episode in the book which would also point the book more towards an adult market. It's bad enough reading it as an adult.

The Impossible Horse was published by Evans Brothers Limited in 1957, with a dustjacket and internal illustrations by Maurice Tulloch. He provided a frontispiece and seven internal illustrations.

The book's first paperback appearance was as a Green Dragon book, now under Christine Pullein-Thompson's own name, and published by Granada in 1972. The Green Dragon books were aimed at readers of 12–15, so presumably publishers had grown a little less queasy in the time since the book first appeared. It kept the internal Tulloch illustrations, but had a new illustrated (and uncredited) cover. Further printings appeared in 1974 and 1976.

There were no further editions until the one you are reading.

ALSO BY CHRISTINE PULLEIN-THOMPSON

And available from Jane Badger Books

David and Pat

The First Rosette

The Second Mount

Three to Ride

The Impossible Horse

JANE BADGER BOOKS

Jane Badger Books is dedicated to bringing back classic pony fiction, some of which has been out of print for over 50 years. Authors available include:

Caroline Akrill

Joanna Cannan

Victoria Eveleigh

Ruby Ferguson

Patricia Leitch

Patience McElwee

Marjorie Mary Oliver & Eva Ducat

Hazel M Peel

Christine Pullein-Thompson

Diana Pullein-Thompson

Josephine Pullein-Thompson

———

www.janebadgerbooks.co.uk

Printed in Great Britain
by Amazon